The Ticket

By

Heather Grace Stewart

The Ticket

By Heather Grace Stewart

Copyright 2016 by Heather Grace Stewart, Graceful Publications
Edited by Jennifer Bogart Jaquith
Books design by Morning Rain Publishing

ISBN: (digital) 978-0-9918795-7-1
ISBN: (print) 978-0-9918795-6-4

Also by this Author

Strangely, Incredibly Good
Remarkably Great (sequel to *Strangely, Incredibly Good*)
The Ticket
The Friends I've Never Met (digital screenplay)
Caged
Three Spaces
Carry On Dancing
The Groovy Granny (Kindle, Kobo; audio version on iBooks)
Leap
Where the Butterflies Go

More info: www.heathergracestewart.com

All Books Available At: www.author.to/hgracestewart

Dedication

For Kayla, because you told me, "You'd better get going on that, pronto, Mommy!" when I told you about my idea for this novel. Thanks for the big shove, sweet girl!

For Bill, my love and my office technician! Thanks for all the support, emotional and technical, and for believing in me on the days that I don't.

Thanks

A self-published author is nothing without her readers and her creation software.

Thanks to my wicked Wattpad readers, my wonderful Wordpress readers, and Canva, for keeping me creating and for making it fun. Thanks also to my amazing Facebook and Twitter followers.

Allie

Chapter

One

"Ouch! *Mother fucker!*"

"Shhh! You'll scare all the patients in the waiting room!"

My OBGYN sounded ashamed as she said it, and yet, she kept on digging and scraping like a miner searching for gold. I lay back and tried to focus on the white ceiling. It had a bold blue sticker on it: Follow Me On Facebook. I moaned, but not from the pain. I heard the cold *clink clink* sound of tongs hitting a metal bowl. What did that make my vajayjay, a cobb salad?

Don't you think the patients outside should know that you're ripping my insides out? I wanted to scream at her; instead, I bit my tongue, pushed my feet further into the stirrups, and did a series of those tiny breaths I learned nearly two decades ago in Lamaze. Breathe in, then out, out, out, out. Try not to panic or it will make it hurt more. You are not going to die from a pap and an IUD replacement! Except, why is the doctor's face so grim?

Dr. Halo stared at me a moment, then back into that dark place, and then she started cursing to herself quietly. Most of what she muttered was undecipherable to me.

"Murble, murble, marshmallow brains! You forgot to tell me you had a tilted uterus! Damn! I'm using the wrong tools!"

I bolted up, but she pushed my chest, forcing me back down, ripping my skimpy paper gown up the backside in the meantime. "Not yet," she said, and I felt a painful pinch.

"There! Isn't it beautiful?"

She was dangling the T-coil in front of my face with an inane grin on her face. I looked around for cameras. This had to be some prank show. It had to be. Jimmy Kimmel was going to walk through those doors laughing, tell me to get some clothes on, and offer me a luxury weekend at a resort in Maui, just for being a good sport.

It had been my idea to get an IUD after the birth of our second daughter. A vasectomy felt so permanent in the beginning and neither of us wanted it, despite that Dan had told me numerous times he didn't want any more kids. In the end, he never had the surgery because he never got around to it. As I laid there in agony, having one IUD removed and another inserted, I wondered, why bother? It wasn't like we were having sex anymore. Things dried up for us in the bedroom years ago. I was just trying to be responsible, and you're supposed to replace it every five years. Still, it was weird when I found that condom in Dan's suitcase this morning. He swore it was an ongoing prank between him and Brian, his longtime boss, but did men over 40 seriously still play frat school jokes like that?

"One condom. Allie, come on, what am I going to do with one condom? If I were cheating on you, I'd buy boxes."

"Thanks, that's consoling." I tried to chuckle and brush the whole thing off by offering to make him pancakes. I felt like a royal bitch for not trusting him.

"Never mind about the pancakes—I have to get to work early."

"But you just got back from LA."

"Tax time. You know how busy it gets. See you at counseling."

The Ticket

We'd been going to see our marriage counselor Lori for almost a year, but clearly, it hadn't done much for our marriage. I still had trust issues, and Dan wasn't even kissing me goodbye as he raced out the door.

"Yup. She said she had a full morning, but could see us at six. I'll put the girls' meals in the fridge, and they can just heat it up. Maybe we can grab a bite after," I said.

"Maybe. Bye."

Getting Dan to go to counseling had been like pulling teeth, but after a few weeks, he seemed more comfortable and was really opening up in our sessions. The three of us were even laughing together.

"Okay, get dressed." A low female voice startled me out from my deep thoughts, and my dreams of Jimmy Kimmel sweeping me off my feet and onto a tropical island were shattered. "I'll see you in six months, unless you hear from us earlier."

Once I'd dressed and set my next appointment, I sat in the car a few minutes, massaging my lower abdomen and feeling badly about how I'd treated Dan. He'd just come home last night, and we'd already bickered twice. Dr. Halo's office is right around the corner from where Dan works. I decided to swing by and drop off a mocha Frappuccino, his favorite. Dr. Lori said it's the little things that can bring the spark back into a marriage. I had to try harder. Maybe then Dan would try, too.

Dan's large accounting firm had one main receptionist, Stacey, in a building of sixteen offices. We'd bonded over everything from our children having chicken pox, to their first dates and proms. She was very sweet. This morning she was applying mascara when I rushed past her desk, a mocha Frapp in my hand. I'd already inhaled mine, with extra whipped cream and a couple Advil, and was feeling much better.

"Oh sweetie, he has someone in there…" Stacey stood up.

"It's okay, I'll just give him this and be on my way."

I opened his door. There was already a mocha Frapp on his desk…

… Along with a woman in a short skirt that was hiked up to her hips. She sat motionless, her backside to me. His hands were on her hips; his groin had been pushing against hers. When his eyes met mine, he pulled away from the woman.

"Allie. Allie, it's not what you think." He was as white as the boxers peeking out of his open fly.

The woman jumped off the desk, then slowly turned toward me. I gasped and dropped Dan's Frappuccino all over the carpet.

Lori.

"Your mouth was on our marriage counselor's mouth. Are you giving her CPR with your fly undone?"

"Allie. It's been over a while. You know that." He wiped bright pink lipstick from his mouth and looked at me, shame and tears in his eyes.

"It wasn't over! I brought you a fucking Frappuccino! It wasn't over!"

I raced out of the room, determined not to let them see me cry.

Chapter

Two

One Year Later

"Ouch! *Mother fu...*"

I'm about to scream a string of profanities, but my boss, Jed Rubicon, is standing beside my desk, glaring at me, so I bite my tongue as I hop on one foot, massaging the other.

"I mean, *Mother Theresa*!" I wince and force a smile.

Jed gives me a funny look.

My foot is throbbing. I was in such a hurry to get to my office, I didn't notice someone had placed a pile of folders and papers to recycle on the floor just outside the door. I managed to gracefully step over them, but then tripped at the last minute, hitting my foot on the corner of the filing cabinet. Smooth. So embarrassing. Jed witnessed the entire fiasco.

"You're late again, Allie." Jed frowns at me, his silver-haired brows furrowing. He's a name partner at Rubicon, March & Morgan.

"I know, and I'm sorry. The subway was delayed," I say, knowing full well that's not a good enough excuse when you're female and working for the most senior partner in one of the top law firms of the city. My commute from our home in Briarwood has been the same for five years: take the F from Briarwood-Van Wyck one stop, then transfer to the E train at Union Turnpike. The subway ride is 30 minutes when there is no train traffic or other delays, but this morning I hit 'snooze' twice, and there was no Dan to shake me awake. I haven't been able to get my shit together since the divorce.

I place my laptop case on my chair and pull out a folder. Please let this help the situation. Please.

"I was poring over these last night, and I think it might help us with the Dalton v. Steiner renewable energy appeal?"

Jed opens the file and silently reads the section I've highlighted on the top two pages. "This is excellent work. Excellent, Allie. I'll show these to Don. We'd like you to work on this case with Joan. Try not to be late again, okay?" he says as he leaves, not bothering to close my office door behind him.

I was holding my breath the whole time Jed was speaking. I release a sigh of relief, then sit back in my brown leather chair, letting it swirl around so I can look out at the cityscape.

Downtown New York, on a grey Monday morning, dirty December snow piled up on the sidewalks. December snow is so much prettier that first time it falls: fluffy and full of Christmas promise. Now it's just gross brown slush that reminds me of my failed attempts to make Gram's homemade Christmas gravy look and taste like hers. Somehow, it also reminds me I haven't done any shopping yet, and Christmas is this Friday.

I don't want to think about Christmas. I'll be a single parent this time, and still not partner. I thought after seven hard-working years here they'd finally consider me, but Joan told me she didn't feel I was ready yet.

Ready? I've billed 2400 hours a year for the last decade, missed half a dozen funerals, and haven't taken a week's vacation in three years. I'm well-respected by all the other associates. Even my jerk of an ex said I was a shoe-in for partner this year. When I make gaffes like being late this morning, though, it's like I go ten steps backward—for the record, I walked in at 8:05 a.m., and I worked until 8:15 last night. I feel like Don, and especially Jed, are poised and ready to mark one more strike against me on their secret tabulated system: operation oust Allie.

I've never worked on a case with either of them. They're always making me work with the one female partner in this firm, Joan Morgan. Do they think only women can work together? I don't get it. I also don't like Joan. She's always trying to trip me up. It's like she doesn't want any other woman at this firm attaining what she's achieved. We have enough obstacles in our way in the workplace. Why can't women build each other up instead of tearing each other down?

I've noticed Joan only wants to work on the corporate cases with the big players. I know I need those kinds of cases for exposure, but the reason I went into law was to help the little guy. I want to help those wrongfully accused and people screwed by companies.

Remember that woman whose thighs were burned by McDonald's coffee in 1994? She became a joke around the world, an overused example of a frivolous lawsuit, but if you read up on the case, *Liebeck v. McDonald's Restaurants,* you learn the poor woman was 79 years old and that, in fact, her entire pelvic area was severely burned. She required skin grafting for her third-degree burns, but she couldn't afford to pay her hospital bills and felt she should also be awarded for her pain and suffering, so she sought legal help.

Some joke. The jury applied the principal of comparative negligence and found that McDonald's was 80 percent responsible for the incident. Liebeck was only 20 percent at fault. Although there was a warning on the coffee cup, the jury decided that it was neither large enough nor sufficient. They awarded Liebeck $200,000 in compensatory damages, which was then reduced by 20 percent to $160,000.

I wish I could tackle that kind of case. I want to help clients who can't afford to pay a lawyer, but Joan and Jed snap up the few pro bono cases they're required to take on. "Billables, little girl. Focus on the billables." That's Jed's daily mantra. I should sue him for calling me a little girl all the time. For fuck sake. I'm 42! The three of them are only ten years older, but they act like that puts them in an exclusive club. Once, I told Jed I didn't like him calling me that. He just laughed.

A laugh. A good, long, belly laugh. That's what I need this morning. Everything went downhill when Dan called me at 7:35 while I was running to catch the subway. I haven't smiled since.

I swear he does it on purpose. He calls when he knows I'm rushing off somewhere, in public, or with the girls so I can't call him a delusional douchebag again.

I realize name calling is highly immature, but I think I'm entitled. In fact, that's mild, considering he left me for our marriage counselor. I wish I hadn't picked up the call this morning, but it didn't have his distinctive "ASSHOLE!" ringtone my best friend Trixie bought me a few weeks after our divorce was finalized. It's hilarious, but it gathers a lot of stares from passersby if it's on its loudest setting.

"ASSHOLE CALLING! AN ASSHOLE is calling! You don't have to pick up!" a woman's voice calls from out of my coat pocket whenever it's Dan.

I know the ringtone is crude. I know not all men are assholes. Some women are assholes. But my ex is indeed an asshole, and the ringtone makes me giggle when not much else has this year, so I've kept it.

This morning, though, the ringtone didn't make me laugh. It was a *bleeep, bleeep* sound, like I'd been floating in the pool and just dropped my phone in, which I wouldn't mind doing some days. Some days, I am far too connected.

I picked up.

"Allie James," I answered, short of breath from running in two-inch heels. I wish I'd just worn my sneakers. A woman in a matching red hat and scarf glared at me; I suppose for managing to say my name while sprinting in cute shoes. I grinned in spite of her and kept on running toward my stop.

"Al, it's me. We need to talk about Christmas."

"Dan! What number are you using?"

"It's Lori's. I'm with Lori. Can't find my cell, so I used hers. Anyway—"

"Why do you have to rub it in my face at *fucking early in the morning*? Why?"

"Al, I'm not rubbing it in your face. Life just happens. I didn't plan this. You know that."

"I know one thing: she planned it. I just read about this similar case in London, where the marriage therapist was actually sued for manipulation. I could sue, you know. I should sue."

"But you won't. You're not that woman. You're too kind-hearted. Besides, she lost her license, you got the house, what more do you want?"

"Dan, if kind-hearted translates into letting you walk all over me, you're wrong. We're not going to let our girls suffer because of our mistakes. Got that?"

"Yea, well that's why I called. I wanted to see if the girls can join me and Lori and Mandy at her parent's cabin upstate over Christmas. Maybe for a week, so you can still celebrate New Year's with them after? You can tell the girls Stacey and Stephanie are joining us, and it has a hot tub."

An entire week, alone. When the girls were little, I'd have put down the phone and done multiple cartwheels over it. Just getting a chance to poop on the toilet without being interrupted was rare back then. But now? Now they're 17 and 19, and when they aren't arguing over who gets the car or the shower, we have a lot of good times together. This plan would leave me all by myself over the holidays.

A few weeks ago, when we were discussing how we'd manage Christmas, they both admitted that they wanted try to forgive their father and get back to how things were a year ago. They'd avoided him and Lori for half the year and were only now starting to socialize with him on weekends. Lori's daughter, Mandy, is a year older than Emma, and the three girls have been getting along rather well, considering the circumstances.

"Lori is okay once you get to know her," our youngest, Emma, said after they returned from dinner that night at Lori and Dan's new apartment. "We did Wii dance with Stacey, and Lori had homemade pizzas for us!"

"She really does love him, Mum," Kayleigh added with a slight frown. "They just went about the whole thing wrong."

None of that was easy for me to hear. That they were enjoying Lori's cooking, but were never big fans of mine sent my emotions over the top. I excused myself and went to bawl my eyes out in our half bathroom. I'm by no means ready to forgive Dan, but if they can find forgiveness in their hearts, I'm not going to stand in their way. He's their father.

What would I do with myself with a week alone? Certainly the girls would want to spend Christmas Day with me, but a ski trip with a new friend their age would be hard for me to one-up for the holidays. I could feel my heart beating hard and fast inside my chest cavity, and it wasn't because I'd just missed my train.

"Dan, I'm late for work. We'll talk about this later. And next time, call me on your own fucking phone."

I turned off the cell, slipped it into my coat pocket, and took a firmer grip of the hand rail. The 20-something thin, blonde woman beside me with bright red lipstick looked down, as though she hadn't heard the conversation. Excellent. Being pitied by a Taylor Swift lookalike just made me feel shittier.

Chapter Three

I'm hiding under my desk, giving myself a once-over in my compact mirror. I'd better not meet Mr. Right, or even Mr. Tonight, because I look like I've been hit by a truck. My mascara has run, and I don't have time to do anything but lick-and-rub. Gross, but efficient. My blue-grey eyes look tired, and my blonde hair could use a good cut. My fair skin needs some lipstick, but I've tried to apply it at my desk before, and everyone walking down the hall sees me through my office's glass walls, whether I'm under my desk or not. I don't feel like being teased right now. I'll just have to get straight to work, after a cup of coffee and a quick check on my email. I shove the compact in my purse and sit back up.

I wonder if Trix has written me her daily email yet. We never did get into texting, although we exchange them here and there. We used to write post cards and snail-mail letters in college, and we still love exchanging long notes. I hope she's sent me one today, because I need a good, long laugh. What else are BFFs for? I wake up my computer and open my email.

I can't help but grin when I realize she's sent me an early Christmas e-card. Oh, Trix, my dear old friend, you are the bomb. I turn up the speakers, not too loud, just enough to hear it, and press play. If it's from Trix, this should be good.

Jib Jab are the first words that pop up on screen, and then the song, *All I Want for Christmas Is You*, starts spilling out from my desktop speakers. I start to giggle. Three little elves with skinny legs and huge heads are dancing across my screen. They're doing the can-can, their giant bobble heads bopping along to the beat. I do a double take, because now I recognize the dude in the middle.

It's Jed. She's pasted Jed's head on a dancing Jib Jab elf! Don's the one beside him. And, oh, for the love of St. Nick! I cannot pee my pants at my desk, I must contain my laughter, but there's Joan, prancing around in an ugly green collared top and red mini skirt.

Bless you, Trix. You've turned my least favorite colleague into a dancing elf.

I wipe the tears that are forming at the corners of my eyes and lower my head so no one can see the size of my smile. Smiles are rare at this law firm, especially at nine in the morning, unless we're raising champagne glasses.

I can feel a presence at my right side. No, no, no, this isn't happening. How did Joan creep in here so fast? I manage to cut the sound fast enough so she can't make out the tune and hide the window so it keeps playing, but she can't see the card on my screen.

Joan lets out a deep sigh, stares at my screen, and gets right to business.

"Allie. I've ironed out the details of the Save More-Good Groceries merger. I want you to go over these carefully."

I open up the folder and read the first document, clenching my teeth as I try to remain professional. "But, Joan, this isn't what I suggested. My way was going to save five thousand people their jobs. This is… definitely not that."

"No, it's not. Your way was much too… helpful, Allie. We aren't in the business of helping others. We do what our clients want us to do."

"But, all those people will lose their jobs right after Christmas! Imagine the debt they'll get into."

"That's not our problem. I thought you understood how these things work by now?"

"Sure, I do. I'm just starting to realize I don't like how they work, and I…" I hesitate, then collect my thoughts. "I think I can do something about it."

"Not on my watch, and not on Jed or Don's. Allie…" She bends over, leaning on my desk, and accidentally brushes her hand across my wireless mouse. As soon as she swipes it, the window I'd hid slides up and across the screen. My dancing law partners resume getting jiggy with it in beautiful 3-D color.

NOOOOOOOOOOOOOO! I'm screaming inside my mind, because I can't possibly open my mouth to speak, or even breathe right now. I imagine myself jumping out this window. Escaping this moment. Exactly *now*.

Joan watches the bobble-head version of herself slap her own behind and looks away from the screen. Her expression is grim, her lips pursed, her eyes narrowing and glaring at me.

"So, is this how you spend your billable hours? Making dancing bobblehead versions of the name partners?"

"Actually, no, my friend Trixie made the card. I think she had a digital photo of you all from last year's Christmas party. I swear I didn't…" I'm stammering. I knew I shouldn't have opened my mouth.

Joan slams her hand down on the desk, hard. "Allie James, you need to grow up and decide what you can offer this firm."

"What I can offer you? I've given you two thousand four hundred hours a year for a long time, now, Joan." I stand up. I'm not taking her bullying sitting down. It was just a freaking e-card. She needs to get a sense of humor.

Joan takes a step back, but keeps frowning at me. "That's true. You haven't taken a vacation in three years, have you?"

"No," I say, realizing I probably shouldn't feel proud of this, but I do.

"Jed and I were talking," she says, and I notice her left eye twitching, "and we think you need to take some time off. It hasn't been the easiest year for you, and—"

"Don't treat me like that." I cut her off, clearing my throat. "Like someone to pity. I'm not. I'm handling it all fine. I've been late a few times, but I haven't let you down on one case this year. Not one. I'm reliable. I just need more sleep, but..."

"That's exactly it, though. You need to take a rest. Decide if law is your future. You do good work, but I've never seen you fired up. I want to see passion in your eyes."

I sit down again. "Are you... is this?" I can't get my words out. My palms are sweaty, and my face feels flushed red.

"No, no Allie, we want you at the firm, but it doesn't seem like you want to be here. You're coming in late and making dancing elf partners instead of working."

"I didn't make any dancing elves! I just opened a fucking e-card!" I raise my voice, far too loud, as the words echo out the door and down the hallway.

"Enough. Enough now." She looks at me like my grade one teacher did when I kept accidentally erasing holes in the foolscap paper. "We'll call this a forced vacation. Take five weeks—paid. Come back to us in mid-January, and hopefully, we'll see the old Allie again."

Joan takes her file folder, and my dignity, and walks out of my office. I hold back my tears, but I can't stop shaking. I glance back at my screen. The three elf partners are no longer dancing. Now they're dramatically blowing me kisses, and holding up a sign: THE END.

I flip them the finger. I hope they get run over by Santa's reindeer.

Pete

Chapter

Four

It would be great if I didn't have to wear pants under this desk.

I'd be like one of those guys from that TV show *Sports Night*. Why should I have to wear pants—dress suit pants, at that? No one watching ever sees me from the waist down.

Whew. It's so hot under these damn lights, with me suddenly in the spotlight. I'm reminded of my favorite Gaelic expression: *Iss min-ick a vrish bay-al din-eh a hrone*. Many a time a man's mouth broke his nose. Unfortunately, I'm not allowed to keep my mouth shut right now. Luck of the Irish, my ass. What have I done?

"Our newscast is a little different this afternoon," my colleague, Jessica Legs, says to camera one. Legs is not her real last name, but with legs all the way down to the floor like that, I can't help but call her that. Yup, I know it would be sexual harassment if I said it out loud, but a man's entitled to his own thoughts.

"We're turning the tables and interviewing one of our own, Pete McCarney, our nightly news anchor for the last two years here at NBC.

Pete, last night, you posted a message on your Facebook page. You wrote that you'd planned a trip to six beautiful cities around the world over Christmas, but that you've recently split with your girlfriend of one year, and now you can't get a refund on the ticket. So, you've put out a call for anyone with a valid US passport bearing the name Allison James to come forward, and you'll pay all expenses for her three-week trip.

"The message went viral overnight, and there have been over ten million shares, across Facebook alone. Did you expect that kind of response? And, frankly, is this some kind of joke?" Jessica Legs doesn't look amused. Her cheeks have turned pink, and she's frowning at me.

"No, it's not a joke, and I hope I still have a job." I chuckle and attempt to loosen my tie. It feels like a boa constrictor around my neck.

10 million shares. What the hell have I done? Al is going to be totally pissed at me about this. I thought this through—hell, I even took precautions with NBC and texted the CEO, my buddy Garrett Maklen, about it, but we didn't think it would go viral. I didn't think women would actually want to take this trip with me. I mean, women have told me I'm good-looking, funny, and smart, but to travel the world with someone they've never met? Wait. Did I actually come up with this idea myself, or did Garrett talk me into this? I have to stop drinking those vodka and tonics after work. I'm too old to be drinking at 3 a.m.

"Of course you still have a job—you haven't done anything wrong, but I can say this with certainty: your ex-girlfriend is going to stay your ex-girlfriend." Jessica laughs into the camera.

"Yea, well, she made it quite clear that she doesn't want the ticket, and I asked if I could post on social media about it because the trip is this Saturday. She was fine with it. Neither of us expected this kind of response. I have people from England and Australia named Allison James asking if they can use their passports to join me."

"And can they?"

"No, sadly, it's only going to work if you're an Allison James with a valid US passport."

"Pete. You're a newscaster. You earn a good salary. Why not just forget about the ticket and go alone?"

God, these lights are burning up my face like the Mexican sun! There must be sweat dripping off my earlobes. I wipe my brow and turn to look right into the camera. I'm an award-winning newscaster, damn it. Just because it's getting a little personal, do I have to lose half my bodily fluids on national television? Pull it together, McCarney!

"I think everyone needs a little adventure in their lives, and I kept reporting about people taking wild chances, but I've never really done that. Not once in my life. I've always taken the careful route. Even as a reporter, I shied away from danger and reported on finance.

"So, I had this idea last night, and I ran with it. I didn't foresee that I'd be on the noon newscast today talking about my personal life, that's for sure." I grin, hoping people aren't going to think I'm a schmuck. I sound like a schmuck. Bollocks!

"Are you our next Bachelor? The one with the gorgeous Irish accent?" Jessica grins at me. Good lord. Is that what people think?

"I am a bachelor, and I was born on the Emerald Isle, but I don't think this is going to be anything like that show!"

"I work with you Pete—everyone out there should know—you're nothing but a gentleman."

Jessica smiles at me again, and I feel a wave of relief wash over me. There. Much better. Now she's given the women watching her own vote of confidence.

"Yes, I'm usually a private guy, as you know. What I'm doing here is totally outside my comfort zone, but hey, life is short."

"So, we need to make it clear, you're not trying to reinvent *The Bachelor*."

"Definitely not. Never watched the show. We'll have separate rooms, of course. I'm just offering up a ticket that was going to go unused. It's a three-week trip around the world. I think we could have lots of fun." I smile at the camera and add, "Allison James, wherever you are."

Allie

Chapter

Five

Drinking beer in the bathtub. Why isn't that a thing? I'm making it a thing. Even if it is 3:30 in the afternoon on a Tuesday. Done. It's now an official thing.

I've never seen any magazine articles about the health benefits of drinking a beer in a hot bath, but I'm certain I can google it and come up with something convincing, if someone were to give me a hard time about it. Which they won't, because nobody phones the land line anymore, and to avoid Dan's calls, I turned my cell to text notification only. So they'd never know I'm in here, having a beer in the bath on a Tuesday afternoon, instead of working on a groundbreaking grocery store merger case. I could hit my head and drown in here, and my girls, or Trix, might not find me until Wednesday night. I'd ruin our weekly wine night, and at my funeral, she'd curse my strange obsession with beer and baths.

Stop it. Stop being morbid. This is supposed to be relaxing. I close my eyes, take my right leg and rest it on the edge of the bathtub and submerge the rest of my body in the warm, bubbly water.

Don't think. Is that even possible for me? To just let it all go, and take a rest? To not think about law, or what Jed or Joan need, or what the girls need, or what Dan needs? Crap. Scratch that last one. I'm not supposed to care about him anymore. Why can't I just let it all go?

The uncomfortable lump in my throat is growing larger. Damn it, I don't want to cry anymore, but the tears are falling from my eyes, down my cheeks and neck. I wipe them with the back of my arm, take a long swig of beer, and rest my head back on my soft bath pillow.

I just want to start having fun again. Joan is right. I can't believe it, but she's bang-on. I need to figure out what I'm passionate about because somewhere along the way, while I was taking care of everyone else's needs, I lost sight of my own. What am I passionate about, anyway, besides making sure my girls are alright?

Ping. Ping. I knew this quiet wouldn't last. Nope. I'm staying submerged beneath these heavenly bubbles. What day is it again? Tuesday. It's Tuesday afternoon. So it's probably one of the girls reminding me they're each getting a ride to work after school. I need to check their texts. Maybe their rides fell through.

I wonder, if when I'm 85, I'll still worry whether Em and Kay got to where they were going safely, on time, with everything they needed to bring. "Don't forget your requisition," I've texted Kay before a doctor's appointment, knowing it's clingy, cursing my mothering gene. Does she even appreciate that? I really do need to let go and just be present in my own life for a while.

When I say present, I'm thinking wrap presents all week, spend time with Mum, Dad, Trix, and the girls on Friday, then be present on the sofa for back to back episodes of anything HGTV for the next four weeks. That's my plan, and I'm sticking with it.

I stand up, step out of the bath, wipe the bubbles off my hands with a towel, and grab my cell on the counter to check my texts.

<I heard. I'm here. Let me in when I ring.>

What is Trix doing taking time off work for me? Shit! This is exactly what I don't want. I don't want people making a big deal about this forced vacation. It's embarrassing enough that my colleagues at the firm know what went down. I don't want my friends and family finding out. Trix must have called my office, and someone spilled about it. At least I know she can keep secrets. I don't want my girls worrying about my job security, or worse, Dan rubbing my nose in this.

I race to my closet drawers, slip on panties and a bra, and throw a big t-shirt over my head. It's one from Trix, a joke-gift she got for me from the dental office where she's a hygienist. We spend lots of time watching movies together, and she's always getting me items that play on famous lines. This t-shirt features a large molar and dental tools with the words sprawled across the bottom: You Can't Handle The Tooth.

I simply can't stand the feeling of wet hair. I shake it a little as I towel-dry it, all while running down the stairs. It's something I've told my girls not to do about a million times, and I make a mental note to stop being a total hypocrite, right after this one time.

Trix is looking through the arched glass window on our front door when I get there. She's pouting and holding up a magnum bottle of red wine. I shake my head, chuckling, and open the door.

"Go away."

"Nope. Not leaving you in your hour of need."

"Hour? Try five weeks. Five weeks of need!"

"Don't rub it in. You're on vacation! I'm so jealous." Trix leans in and gives me a long hug. Her jet black hair is slightly damp with snowflakes. It smells like a wet, perfumed dog. A dog that wears Chanel No. 5. I won't say anything, because she's here for me, and she's probably thinking I have beer breath and badly need to floss my teeth.

I take her coat, and she kicks off her boots and hands me the wine. Red Zinfandel. I love this woman. She understands me, and she validates my feelings. It's such a shame I like penises.

"Are we having some now, or are you heading back to work?"

"Actually, I'm taking a late lunch, then Dr. Sabel is closing the office and filling my tooth for me. But, I can have a little. It might make the drilling less painful," she says, following me into the kitchen.

"So that's why you're off work. I feel better now." I pour us each a half glass and hand her the one that says Standing Sun Vineyards.

"Shit. Dan and I celebrated our fifteenth anniversary there. Give me the glass."

"What?" Trix isn't easily offended, but she's possessive about her wine.

"Just give it to me for a sec, so I won't be staring at those words while we talk." I grab another glass, pour her wine in it, and hand it back to her, tossing the anniversary glass in our recycling bin. It smashes as it hits a pickle jar—it's a very satisfying sound, this shattering glass. When I look back up, Trix is frowning at me.

"See, if you still had a fucking therapist, you wouldn't need to do those things," she says. She doesn't look surprised about the broken glass.

"I had one, but she's a little busy doing my ex-husband."

"I came over here to console you, not make things worse." Trix takes my hand and starts to lead me to our comfy living room sofa, but I feel a craving coming on.

"I want Häagen-Dazs with our whine," I say, pretending to sob as I say the 'whine' part. "It's definitely a Häagen-Dazs kind of day."

"If it contains chocolate, I'm in," Trix calls from the living room. When I return, I hand her a pint of Brownies & Cookie Dough and two spoons.

"Sit. Vent. Cry. Or just sit and eat ice cream with your old friend," she says, patting the spot beside her.

I sit down, take a sip of my Zinfandel, and then another. The cherry-blackberry aftertaste is addictive.

"Trix, they don't value me at the firm, and I don't like the way my work makes me feel. I need something new. I know that. But, can I start over at forty-two?"

"Probably not."

That's my Trix, always telling it like it is.

"You can't start over, but you can start anew." She puts down her wine and slaps her hands on her thighs. "Hell, I sound wise! What happened?" She giggles, then takes out her phone and opens her Facebook app. "Anew. Such a great word, and I have an example to underscore my point. This. This would be anew for you."

"Are you trying to rhyme words and be annoying all at once? Facebook? We're seriously going to spend our quality girl time together reading Facebook?"

Trix is ignoring me. She's furiously scrolling, trying to find the post.

"You know the NBC newscaster? That cute young guy? Well, younger than your average newscaster?"

"Oh, um, what's his name, McCarney, right? Pete. Yes, he seems like a pompous ass. What's the point?"

"You think he's an ass? Oh, not good. Well, we can work with that. I think he's clever, and funny, and he's looking to take someone with *your* name around the world. Look!"

"My name? What? What are you talking about? What the fuck is in this wine?" I put down my glass and grab the phone from her hands.

Trix takes a neon green hair scrunchie and pulls her long black hair up into a high ponytail. She's always been a little stuck in the 80s, but that's one of the many reasons why I love her. She leans back into my big animal-print pillow and sighs.

"If you'd just shut your mouth for one blooming minute, sweets, I've been trying to explain it to you. There, that's the post." She points to a photo of Pete McCarney and a bunch of text beneath it. I have to admit, he's sweet eye-candy for this perimenopausal mess. He's wearing a purple tie, a modern, dark-grey shirt, and his sea-blue eyes sparkle so bright, I wonder if this has been photoshopped. Of course it has, dummy, it's on the NBC site. He's their commodity. Don't fall for this, Al. He's probably not what he seems.

But what does this Pete McCarney seem to be? I enlarge the picture, highly aware that Trix is wearing a gloating 'I told you so' smirk beside me. Never mind her, figure this guy out. You're a lawyer. You can figure him out in five seconds.

Sandy brown hair, speckled with bits of grey, broad shoulders, a sexy bit of stubble on his angular jaw. He looks distinguished but not snooty, intelligent, and his eyes look kind. There's also something I can't quite put my finger on behind that mischievous smile. I push away the nagging, gut instinct and my desire to find out what it is. I don't have time for this, and a piece of me fears I don't have the courage.

"So, the story goes that his girlfriend broke up with him a few weeks before their trip around the world. He's good-looking, he's got a great job, we know he's bright, and he's got a ticket with your name on it. It's your ticket, Allie. I just know it."

"Have you lost your fucking mind?" I throw her phone at her, aiming for the pillow on her lap. "No way. I'm not doing this."

Trix catches the phone before it bounces off the pillow, then turns it off. "Come on. You've got this all-men-are-assholes chip on your shoulder, but you can't live like that. It's too heavy a load to carry, and it's wrong."

"I know. I'm just so angry, Trix." I sigh and reach for the ice cream. "We were supposed to be forever."

"Nothing is forever, sweetie. Häagen-Dazs isn't bottomless, we all grow old, and at some point, we all have to say goodbye."

"What about old lovers who die in their sleep and meet up in heaven?"

"I'd like to believe in that, Allie, but I'm just trying to focus on the day to day, here on earth. It's enough to think about."

"Yea. Okay so all men are not jerks. I agree with you on that. I mean, even I've been a jerk… I just didn't let it rip our marriage apart."

"No, but it was close. I remember that year. Your first year of marriage. You thought it was going to be all Martha Stewart weddings, and you were so disappointed you fell for that guy in the law offices next door."

"Jake. Yeah. But it was just lunch. And kissing."

"Just kissing? I'm not one to judge, Al, but a lot of people call that cheating."

"I know, I know. It was a dumb mistake, and I still regret it, but we worked through it. This time was different. We were in counseling for eight months, and he was fooling around with her for six!"

Trix isn't often soft-spoken, but suddenly, her voice gets quiet, and she seems introspective. She takes both my hands in hers and looks right through me.

In a world where it feels like everyone's fallen for their iPhone, sometimes Trix's intensity is too much for me. With no lover in my bed, I've forgotten what actual eye contact feels like. It's like she's looking right through me.

"Al, don't miss out on this. I can feel it in my bones," she says. "It's like a sign or something."

"You know I don't believe in signs, Trix."

"But it's your *name*. You have five weeks off! It's perfect."

"Right. And he could be a rapist. Or a Republican. Or both."

Trix groans. "Oh Allie, that was awful, even for you! Not every guy who tries something outside the box is dangerous, or stupid. I like the sound of this guy. Keep an open mind!"

"Yeah, well, it hasn't been the best day. My mind closed around nine fifteen this morning."

"Just go to the interviews. He's offering a round-trip ticket to six outstanding cities you've never seen. London. Prague. Rome. Bangkok, Marrakech, and Cusco!"

"I'm exhausted already." I let go of her hands and grab my wine again.

"Come on. Think of the adventures you'll have!"

"Adventure. That's one word for it. The other one is ludicrous."

Trix takes her spoon and digs into her ice cream. I know her. She's looking for a chunk of cookie dough.

"I know you're thinking about it. I got you thinking about it." She grins.

I say nothing, but hit her over the head with my pillow, hard. She retaliates with a larger pillow and a chuckle that turns into the ridiculous snort-laugh I've heard and loved for thirty years. For a few lovely, lingering minutes, we're giggling twelve-year-old girls again, in a place where everything is possible—where carefree afternoons stretch out into one another and deep sleep always comes easy.

Pete

Chapter
Six

<How can 20 women named Allison James be so different? This is taking forever>

<Just pick one, dufus, ur not marrying her. Ur traveling with her>

I put my cell back down on the news desk and my head in my hands. Garrett's quick text reply makes me feel like I'm being too picky, but three weeks with the wrong woman would be disastrous. We'll be elbow to elbow on an airplane. Passing each other milk and sugar at breakfast. At least in a marriage, you can hide out in your garage, or your office. Not that I actually know much about marriage; I've never been brave enough to find out.

At least I know what I don't want. She can't be afraid to get dirty, to take risks, to miss meals so that we can witness something awe-inspiring. She can't be attached to high heels, a schedule, or her cell phone. She can't smoke or use extremely foul language.

Jeez, I'm sounding terrifyingly similar to my mother with those last two. Better keep them on the list, though, because if I jotted those down without thinking much, they must be important to me. Al once said I over-analyze everything and that it made me miss out on opportunities. Maybe she was right.

I've another hour before they'll need to start setting up the news desk for our Wednesday noon hour report. Garrett let me use the desk for interviews, but suggested I take this week off as anchor, in addition to my upcoming vacation weeks, since there's a lot of media attention on me right now. I'm hoping it dies down in a few weeks, and I'll be taken seriously as an anchor again in January. Tabloids are already running with headlines like, *News Man Looks for Love* and *Ticket to Love*, which make me want to upchuck my breakfast burrito. I specifically said this was not a remake of *The Bachelor*, but, of course, they zeroed in on that and reported the opposite.

How'd I get myself into this bloody ballsed-up mess? Garrett was convincing—he always is—and for once in my life I felt like taking a risk and switching the routine up. It's been the same dull, organized morning for five years running. I sleep in after anchoring news at eleven, my alarm wakes me at nine, I make myself a breakfast burrito with Monterey jack cheese at nine-fifteen, read two papers, and I'm in the shower by ten thirty. I'm usually at work by noon, even though they don't expect me until two. My colleagues always say I'm married to my job, but this year, standing in a silly paper hat as the ball dropped on January first, I told myself that was going to change.

Al did change the course of everything. When we met, I actually thought I could learn to vary my morning routine, but she never wanted to sleep over. She said she had to walk her dog in the morning. It was fine for the first few months, but then I started to wonder if she was making up excuses to avoid spending time with me. Other women have left toothbrushes and makeup kits at my penthouse. She left no trace of herself here.

I was all set to go on the trip with her, then last week, out of the blue, she tells me she's not into hiking, beach-combing, or anything outdoorsy. We met in a Mountain Equipment store and spent a weekend in a leaky tent last summer, so this was all news to me.

The Ticket

She said she had finally realized she was only trying to please her mother by dating me. Apparently, Mom is never satisfied with Al's life choices, but she went to the fridge and opened champagne upon learning she was dating 'that adorable nightly news anchor.'

Pleasing the mother. That again. Perhaps I should just skip a generation and start dating the moms. I can't believe I was considering asking Al to move in with me after Christmas.

I sigh out loud, take a sip of my cold coffee, and look down at the list of DON'TS that I typed up early this morning on my tablet. I count ten. There's only one item in the DO column: She has to love strong beer and blue nacho chips with salsa verde.

What is my problem? This reads like I'm looking for a golfing buddy. Shouldn't I know by now what I'm looking for in a woman?

What I'm looking for in a woman. Damn. I've already set myself up for another major blow to the heart, and I'm only just getting over Al. What am I even thinking? This isn't *The Bachelor: Round Trip Ticket.* It's not supposed to be a shot at romance. I'm just looking for a travel companion. Someone to ease my awkward fear of being alone in foreign places. So, why am I imagining the two of us gazing into each other's eyes while drinking Dutch beer by a fire?

Besides, who's to say any of these women are even going to be remotely interested in traveling with me once we meet? Sure, my accent goes a long way as a charm tool, but that worked more in my college years. This is different. I suspect many of these women have been scorned by love, and so have I. We're selective. Hard to please. Al once called me persnickety.

Seven of the 20 women who registered their interest Skyped me from States too far away to attend the interviews. I put on my best *impersnickety* face for my Skype calls. Hell, I even joked about my made up word, but what followed was what kids these days call an epic fail.

To say we didn't click would be an understatement. One of the women ended the call abruptly when I told her I fully expected her to dance along with an indigenous tribe at the *Quyllur Rit'I,* the Snow Star Festival, in Peru. I was joking, of course, but she didn't give me one second to explain. If she can't stand my sense of humor for a few minutes, how would we fare for a few weeks?

My thoughts are interrupted by a *click click click* on the marble floor. I look over to the door and watch as a tall, red-haired woman in a short skirt and three-inch, pink heels walks my way. She's stunning, but she appears to be not a day older than 20. I'd told Garrett my age minimum was 30. His screening process leaves something to be desired.

"Mr. McCarney. I can't believe I'm meeting you!" She approaches the other chair behind the news desk, but instead of taking my hand, she's opening up her arms for a hug.

No, no, no. My—I guess I can't call her mine anymore—Allison has red hair. I know I'm being ridiculous, but I can't travel with another Allie James who bears such a striking resemblance to my ex. The only similarity should be the name.

Also, I don't do hugs with strangers. The past six women who came in here wanted a hug. If I don't feel it, why fake it? I extend my hand and smile at the woman with red hair.

"Hi. Well, I already know your name. Take a seat, and I'll just ask you a few questions."

Allison Number 20 dramatically tosses her hair over her left shoulder, pulls down her skirt, and sits in the second anchor chair beside me.

"Oh, twirly!" She giggles and starts spinning around.

"So, Allison, why did you want to travel to six different cities with me?"

Allison Number 20 grabs the news desk to stop the chair's movement.

"Woah, now I'm dizzy." She giggles again. "Um, I dunno—it sounded cool on my Instagram. Free trip! Right on!" She pumps one fist in the air.

This is off to a good start. She's the daughter I never had.

I put my cell back down on the news desk, and she instantly grabs it. "Hey! Mr. McCarney! Can we check out how many likes your post has now? Last I checked it was at one hundred eighteen thousand four hundred and fifty-six million! Rock on, right?"

"Rock on, indeed." I smile at her, unlock my screen, hand her the cell, and stand up. NBC pays for my phone. It can babysit her for a while.

"Excuse me, but that's all the time I have for today. I still have to squeeze in a few more interviews. Just leave my phone on the desk when you're ready to leave. I have to make a call."

"Make a call? But I... like... Bae! I have your phone!" Her voice reminds me of a dog's squeaky toy.

"I feel like using the landline. Comfort. Old habits die hard and all that."

"Oh, sure. Die Hard. Bruce Willis, right?! Rock on, right!"

I'm trying to remember who I've hurt to deserve the karma that has been this day of ludicrous interviews, but no, I've always been careful carrying others' hearts. The people I've loved have been far clumsier with mine.

It's been a day of whiny women who are all more interested in my position and money than my personality. I can always spot someone with an ulterior motive a mile away, but my exes say I come off as slightly cold and egotistical when I encounter that in a person. Apparently, I shut those people down rather fast, but I don't know how else to react. It's self-preservation. I learned it in first grade when Molly Jack sent me a love note. DO you love me? Check [YES] or [NO]. I loved that she always had *Jos Louis* pastries in her lunch kit, so I checked the [YES] box, and she promptly started copying my work.

So, that was Allison Number 20. Frankly, I wouldn't be able to sit beside any of those women for more than an hour. I'd rather die strapped to my seat, alone in a fiery plane crash.

Maybe they couldn't stand me, either. That one woman did hang up on me. Maybe I am a miserable bugger—I don't know. I could use a beer. What is it, eleven o'clock? Too early. Next week. Next week, when I'm on vacation, the Strong Bow shall flow.

I walk out the studio door and up a flight of stairs, hoping to get some fresh air and a sandwich before the final two interviewees show up. Grabbing my wool coat off the coat rack, I head out into the brisk winter weather. It's snowing hard outside NBC studios, but it's the kind of snow I love: fluffy, and full of promise. A few flakes hit my left eye, and it makes me chuckle because I can't see where the hell I'm going. I take my palm and rub my eye several times, shielding my other eye with my other hand, and continue walking toward Finn's Deli, side-stepping excited Christmas shoppers and, from the sounds of it, a grumbling Salvation Army Santa with bad bell-ringing rhythm.

"Mr. McCarney? Uh, Pete, McCarney? I think we've got a meeting scheduled for about two minutes from now, and I saw you here, so, um, are you still going? Woah, that's some gust of wind!"

She's standing right in front of me, but I can't see her face. I can feel her warm breath on my neck. Oh, in *ainm Dé*, that citrus scented perfume is intoxicating. Her voice is strong yet soft; melodic and engaging, and when it trails off, I wonder if I'm going to lose her.

I step on an icy patch on the sidewalk, and I'm caught off guard. I can't see my way through the storm and start falling forward into her, so I grab onto her shoulders for support.

She thinks I'm offering a hug. My balance is restored, but I won't let go, and to my surprise, neither does she.

We're hugging on a crowded New York City street in a blizzard, and it's the best damn thing that's happened to me in years.

Allie

Chapter

Seven

I'm standing in front of NBC studios in a snowstorm, hugging a pompous ass.

Is my brain on vacation and my body still back in the bath?

Why can't I let go of this man?

Okay, if I'm honest, his arms feel like a thermal blanket in the cold, and his chest and neck smell heavenly. It's like coming home to mulled wine simmering on the stove. What is that scent? A hint of cinnamon, pine needles, sandalwood, and salty sea air blended into the most delicious, aromatic cologne. It's robust and inviting. I wonder how I can ask him about it without sounding like a ditz. "What are you wearing?" would only make me sound like a desperate red carpet correspondent.

Brain, come back! Body, let go. Let him go! Pretend you were helping him gain his balance. He slipped a little, right? Just say that. He's so full of himself, though, he won't admit it.

"You slipped a bit there, everything okay?" I pull away and wonder how he'll respond.

"Yeah, I totally did." He laughs and shakes his head. "I'm assuming you're Allison James." He smiles. "Perhaps I can get your middle name?"

Oh. I didn't expect that. I didn't think he'd care. "Maybe, maybe later," I hear myself stutter. Why do I feel so nervous around him? I only reveal my middle name to a few close friends. It's horrid, embarrassing, and doesn't fit my personality one bit. I think my parents were drunk when they chose it.

"Does it need to match?"

"No, I double checked, the airline just needs first and last names to match," he says. "It's freezing out here. Care to join me inside?"

His accent is even more alluring in person. So what? He's Irish; it's just a different manner of speaking. Nothing to wet my panties over. As I said to Trix as she pushed me into the cab, I'm here for a trip, not a tryst.

Pete opens the heavy glass door for me and gestures for me to go ahead of him.

Alright, so, he just won points in the charm department, but every time I've seen this guy being interviewed on TV, he uses big, rare words, and comes off as holier-than-thou. I'm sure his ego is going to make an appearance soon.

"Right, you'll need this." He pulls out a plasticized guest pass on a string necklace and hands it to me. "The news studio and my office were relegated to the basement a few years ago, while the morning show gets to be on display." He shows me the large room to our left, with its floor-to-ceiling windows looking out onto one of New York's busiest streets. "Ratings. It's all about the ratings." He sighs. "But I'm not sure I'd want a live audience, anyway."

As we make our way down the hallway to a set of tiled stairs, my boots start slipping a little on the floor. They're flat, black fashion boots without good treads. I notice several puddles of melted snow across the steps going all the way down the stairs and no railing to grab onto.

As we stand together at the top of the stairs, Pete looks at me for a moment before speaking.

"Well, I could carry you, but that would be a little too 1870, no?"

I smile up at him. That wasn't bad, considering I've often thought men are damned if they do and damned if they don't when it comes to chivalry these days.

"I think I can manage, but thanks," I say and use his right arm to steady me as I take off my boots and begin walking down the stairs in my favorite bright red socks. As I step around the puddles, missing very few because there are so many, he stands at the top, watching me and chuckling.

"I was about to tell you, Allison, but you move too fast. There's an elevator that goes directly to the studio," he calls down to me. "I'm going to go find a mop and clean this up so you won't slip on your way back up. Go on ahead in, to your right, and sit down. I'll be with you in a minute."

"Okay," I call back up. "Hey," I add, "call me Allie."

Pete McCarney is going to do the janitor's job? That's… surprisingly sweet. Okay, so maybe it was just one time I saw him being interviewed, and he came off as self-important. Once. He also seemed to be an ill-informed feminist. At least he was trying to support women in positions of power; he was just going about it wrong.

I remember now. He was on the popular morning show *Coffee with Carrie*, being asked about his role as nightly news anchor in recent elections. He'd said he'd noticed that the women candidates, like Hillary Clinton, were often criticized for their appearance much more than their male counterparts. He'd said something like, "She should just dress exactly like the men, shirt, tie, pants, and maybe then the media wouldn't make her appearance an issue." He'd likened it to the 1993 Canadian federal election, when the media criticized Kim Campbell for her outfits and that she wore the same earrings almost daily. "It's still an old boys' club, and women need to hit like the boys, if they're hitting to win."

I remember standing up and screaming, "You've got it all wrong, *Bucko!*" to the television screen. Of course, I'd just caught Dan with Lori a few days before, so, the planet's male population was not in my good books. Even Dan's male, castrated cat was cowering in a corner of the kitchen, hiding from me.

I find the news studio easily and head inside the double doors. It's hot in here, no doubt due to the many bright lights hanging from the ceiling. Someone's doing a sound check and three crew guys are rushing around setting up their equipment. I put my guest pass around my neck, smile at them shyly, and sit down at the news desk, but they ignore me and keep going about their business. Oh well. I didn't expect to be the best-looking Allison James who's been here today.

The crew guys are busy taping wiring to the floor, paying no attention to me whatsoever, so I stare into one of the cameras. *This is Allison James with some breaking news...* Naw. I can speak to a jury, no problem, but I'd freeze up on camera. The chair is comfy, though. I notice a white cell phone on the desk, make sure no one's looking, and flip it over. The lock screen is a photo of Pete with some blonde woman, her arms wrapped lovingly around his neck. Oh. I guess he truly is just looking for a travel companion.

So, that's that. My cheeks grow hot with an awkward combination of humiliation and jealousy. I quickly turn the phone back over.

Five minutes pass. My face feels warm, but my feet are soaking wet and cold. I shouldn't have come. What the hell am I doing here? He's not my type. I shouldn't have listened to Trix. The woman's my best friend, but we're so different. She's way more daring than me. Her father's an entomologist, so I guess it's in her genes. She once ate agave worms in Mexico's Xel-ha rainforest. I haven't been farther south than New Jersey. The closest I came to being adventurous was devouring a couple of fried Oreos while caught in a sudden downpour on Hampton beach.

I hear a noise and look over my left shoulder to the far wall. As the small elevator door slowly slides open, I wonder if this man is all that he seems, or more, and if I'll ever get to know him.

Pete steps out of the elevator with a lanky brunette in stilettos on his left arm.

So that's his story. What a player! Now I'm quite sure I don't *want* to get to know him.

Fine. Good. I can go back to drinking beer in the bath and binging on HGTV. I'll convince Joan to take me back after Christmas. My life won't be turned upside down by a man ever again. It's better this way.

Pete

Chapter

Eight

"So this is it. This is the studio."

I shake my left arm profusely, hoping Allison Number 22 will get the message and let go. I need to get back to Allie No Middle Name. She's independent, quirky, and drop-dead gorgeous.

Meanwhile, Number 22 accosted me while I was mopping the stairs.

"Oh, Pete McCarney, aren't you the most adorable thing since sliced bread!"

I wanted to say sliced bread isn't adorable, or even rocket science, although it was sorely missed in 1943 when U.S. officials imposed a short-lived ban on sliced bread as a wartime conservation measure, but I didn't have time. The pushy brunette wrapped her arms around my waist and planted a wet one on my lips. Long. Hard. Intolerable. Her mouth tasted like stale cigars. I didn't want to find out why.

Number 22 takes a few strides across the studio floor, stopping and turning dramatically like a runway model, then posing right in front of the mark our weather person uses. It's deliberate and annoying.

"Do you need a new weather girl, Petie? I've been dreaming of doing the weather all my life." She flutters her eyelashes and does some strange, sulky move with her mouth.

I think she might be imitating a pouty trout, but in a leather skirt and heels. I bite the side of my cheek to keep from laughing at the idea of this pouty trout bimbo guest starring on Sponge Bob. This is where my mind goes when I'm bored and not aroused.

Aroused. Allie. Oh no, Allie. I need to get to Allie.

I look over and give her a small wave. She's sitting at the news desk, looking annoyed. If her eyebrows move down her face any farther, they'll take the place of her nose. *Ifreann na Fola,* I have to do something. We were getting along so well.

"Allison, I'm afraid I have another interviewee waiting for me, and she's been waiting a while. I think I learned enough about you, and your seven sisters, in that painstakingly slow elevator ride down here. You'll get a call if I decide you get the ticket, okay?" I put my hand at her lower back—a move I prefer to use with women I actually hope will stick around—and guide her straight to the studio doors.

"The ticket? Oh right! Sure. I mean, yeah, who wouldn't want to travel around the world with you?" She flashes me her perfectly white teeth as she sweeps her left arm dramatically outward. "Unless, of course, there's a cold front that comes in from the west, with temperatures dropping more than fifteen degrees within the first hour."

"Right. Sure." I've really had enough. "Allison, just watch tomorrow's newscast to find out who I'm traveling with, okay?"

She pouts again, and I think of sending her home with fish food. Before she exits, she turns dramatically once again and frowns at Allie. "I wish you luck. I hear there were a *lot* of applicants. *A lot.*"

I make my way back to the news desk as fast as I can.

"Seven sisters, huh? So, what is this, speed dating?" Allie says. I can't gauge her expression for sure, but I'd say she's more than a little pissed off at me. Okay, McCarney, you can fix this. Give her something good to chew on.

"I try not to do anything involving women quickly, except apologizing," I say and sit down in my chair beside her.

Allie bites her lower lip. I'd say she's trying to avoid a grin and a response. What a firecracker. I think she's actually enjoying this.

"Here." I hand her a dry pair of black socks. "Sorry that whole thing took a few minutes. I went to see Annette in makeup and dress, and sure enough, she had clean socks, plus an array of strange hats and hairpieces. If you want, later, we could sign the Declaration of Independence."

I pull out the white wig I've had behind my back and try it on for size.

Finally, she's laughing. God. I love how her left eye slightly widens like that. It's like it has a mind of its own.

She's turning around in her chair, studying all the cameras on the floor.

"Oh, Mother *fuuucker.* Are you filming this? You can't be filming this!"

Right. I'm going to have to cross off 'uses foul language' on my DON'T list. So what? Coming from her, it's more comical than offensive. She's what, five foot two? At least a foot shorter than me. She's not about to sport gold chains, go highjack a car, and beat someone up in prison, but it's obvious that when she says 'Mother fucker,' she means business. She's strong enough to stand her ground. I love that. I wonder what she does for work.

"No, no of course not. It's just that I didn't want strange women in my home, and there's a window of time before the next broadcast. We thought we'd do the selection process here. Speaking of work, what do you do?"

"Look. Mr. McCarney. This is feeling a little Hugh Hefneresque, and I didn't bring my bunny ears."

"Please, call me Pete. And I'm not trying to emulate Hugh Hefner. I don't even own a pipe. Or a robe."

She's standing up. Don't go! Allie, please. Please don't go.

"Go ahead and make jokes, but I don't find it funny that you're setting women up, here. You're going about this elaborate ruse to find the perfect woman to travel with, when you've clearly got someone else waiting for you at home."

"Ruse? Clearly a ruse, hmm? And how is that clear to you, Allison Wont-tell-me-her-middle-name James?" The crew looks my way. It's rare for anyone at work to hear me raise my voice. She's completely thrown me off-balance.

Allie looks at the crew, then speaks in an annoyed whisper. "Your phone made it quite clear. You just left it sitting here, on the news desk, so I couldn't help but notice the woman cuddling up to you in this picture." She holds up my cell and shows me the shot Mum recently took of me and Eve.

"That's my sister, Eve."

She's blushing. "Oh. Your sister… Eve. She's pretty."

"Yes, she is, and clever. She beats me at Scrabble every time. Do you make it a habit to check out people's cell phones?"

"Well. Yes. I think you can tell a lot about a person by their cell phone," she says.

"Then I'll have to take a look at yours, and you can take a look at mine." Realizing my mistake immediately, I flush bright red. "Not like that!"

"Mr… Pete." She ignores my mistaken innuendo and looks straight at me. Straight into me. "While I was waiting for you and the Red Sea to part again, I remembered an interview you did on *Coffee with Carrie*. I want to ask you what you meant about women dressing more like men for their campaigns. Surely you weren't suggesting that women need to pretend to be something they're not, just to beat men in elections?"

Woah. What did I say: Firecracker. I get up and offer her my hand.

"If we're going to talk feminism and politics, I need beer. What do you say? Should we continue this at Strange Brew? We could get some lunch, too. I'll call us a cab."

Allie looks down at my phone—at the photo of me and Eve. She looks back up at me, her left eye completely covered by one long, thick strand of blonde hair. I want to sweep it off her face and kiss her, hard.

I put my hand down because after seven long seconds, she's not taking it.

"Okay," she finally answers. "But I'm buying."

Allie

Chapter

Nine

I can't believe I agreed to this. Now I'm grabbing brewskies with the guy.

This has got to be some sort of mental break. Dan cheated on me, my firm put me on forced vacation, we ran out of ice cream at home, and I finally lost it.

Well, hell, if I'm crazy, at least let me see six of the most interesting cities in the world before they lock me up.

I should probably tell Pete that I didn't apply for the free trip on Facebook. I'm not an official applicant because I didn't want to post my name until I spoke with him. In fact, I hope I don't have to make anything public at all. How these other women can be so open about their travel plans, I don't know, but I can't. Trix called to find out when and where the interviews were, and I just showed up at the time slot they suggested.

Pete holds open the building's glass door, and we walk out onto the busy street. The snow has slowed, and it feels warmer out, too. I look over at his profile as we start down the small set of stairs. Damn. He's very tall and even better looking in person than on camera. It's a shame they have to cake all that makeup on his face. I like how he holds his body. Usually tall people hunch over a little, but he has a relaxed, confident stance.

"Pete! Pete! Over here! Is she the one?"

A man holding a camera with a very long lens is snapping photo after photo of us. Two more men with cameras are behind him.

"The chosen one?" one of them calls out with a guffaw and snaps more images.

Pete stands in front of me, shielding my face from the paparazzi.

"Stop it! Leave her alone," Pete shouts at the men and stays blocking me. "Taxi!" he calls and whistles for the nearest cab. A yellow NYC taxi pulls up a second later, and Pete opens the back door to let me in. He slides in beside me and slams the door.

"Strange Brew, please, but can you lose anyone following us?" he asks the cabbie.

"Sure thing, Mr. Pete," the cabbie replies.

"God, that was intense," I say.

"Allie, I am so sorry. I should have warned you. I didn't think they were on the story yet."

"Story? We're a story now?"

"Could be," he smiles, "if you're okay with that. I wasn't interested in the other Allies as a travel companion. But you... you're different."

I hesitate a second before responding, looking out my window at the people bustling about on the snowy sidewalk. They look tired and stressed, like they're going somewhere they don't want to go. Sometimes I think humanity is trapped inside an alien family's giant snow globe, and they give it a shake it every now and then, just for kicks.

"The other Allies! This is surreal. I can't believe I'm doing this." I laugh nervously, and he chuckles along with me.

"It's weird for me, too, you know. A good weird, though."

"I didn't even apply for this. I just showed up. Now my kids might see me with you on their Instagram before I even decide if I'm going. I still have unanswered questions."

"You've got kids? I want to hear about them. And, ask me anything," he says as the car comes to a halt. He hands the cabbie two twenties and opens the door.

"I have two teenage girls, and I think we need to get inside." I step out, anxiously looking around for the paparazzi.

"It's okay, Allie, I think we've lost them, for now. Follow me," he says, pulling the gold handle on the heavy wooden front door of Strange Brew pub.

"If I joined you on the trip... would they stalk us everywhere?" I ask as I follow him into the low-lit, quiet pub. There are only about a dozen people in here, but the atmosphere is upbeat. There's some classic rock playing in the background. The only wall that isn't oak paneled is covered in framed, signed images of famous customers. There must be at least 100. Johnny Carson. The Irish Rovers. Oh, and right there, of course, Pete McCarney. I try not to stare at it. I don't succeed.

"God, no. It's just a hot topic right now. It will die down. They'll probably only interview us once the trip is over. They'll want to know about the cities we visited, and if and when we almost killed one another," he says as he points out a booth for us.

"Do you think we will? Kill each other, I mean?"

"I'll probably hire bodyguards to stand outside my room, just to be safe." He smiles at me. "You were rather irked about me and my sister, Eve. People know not to mess with you, don't they?"

"My ex-husband and partners might say otherwise. I'm on a forced vacation from my firm," I say as we slide into the maroon, leather-seated booth. "Personality clash with the female partner." How does he get me to open up like this? I wasn't going to tell anyone but Trix.

"You're a lawyer. That's cool. What kind?"

"Corporate stuff, mostly. I've been working on a merger." I pick up my Strange Brew coaster and fiddle with it. He hands me the drink menu.

"Thanks. Yeah, I'm not happy at the firm. I've been doing nothing for years but attempting to make partner. Eating, sleeping, breathing partner. I need to try something new."

"You could start with white beer. Ever tried that?" The bubbly waitress jumps right into our conversation. "Hey Pete. Nice to see you again," she says, and I wonder if that's going to happen everywhere we go. Wait, what? I'm sounding rather committed to this trip. Well, I can't let him know that yet. He has to clear up a few uncertainties for me first.

"I haven't had red beer in a while; I'll try the one you have on tap," I reply, and Pete orders the white one.

"You want some food with that?" the waitress asks us.

"Yeah, the BLT looks great," I answer. "And can you bring us a bowl of chips and salsa while we wait? Green salsa, if you have it?"

"Fettucine alfredo, thanks," Pete adds.

As the waitress leaves, Pete breaks into a wide grin. It's gorgeous, but I don't know what I did to deserve it.

"You like chips, green salsa, and beer. My kinda gal."

"Pete. I thought this trip was… Okay. Here's the thing. I'm just out of my marriage, and it was a mess in the end. I'm not *looking*," I say emphatically. There. That should do it.

"I just complimented your snack choices, Allie, I wasn't proposing marriage." He's still grinning at me. Somehow, without saying one word, he makes me feel beautiful. It's unnerving.

"Good, because I hardly know a thing about you. What about the women in politics issue? Can you clear that up for me?"

"Look," Pete takes a sip of his beer, then puts it down, "a lot of times, the media takes sound clips totally out of context. I remember that day. I was being sarcastic. I was trying to express how the media scrutinizes women unfairly based on their appearance—hair, skirts, heels, earrings—during campaigns, but also expects women to balls-up and be just like men. I sarcastically suggested women start dressing like men to compete with them. I believe the next thing I said was, 'Do you honestly expect that? That's ludicrous.' But *Entertainment Now*, pathetic attempt at journalism that they are, cut that part out.

"I would never dare tell a woman how to dress, or how to act. Especially not one who's clever and brave enough to run for office. On the other hand, I'd like to tell the media where to go." He picks his beer up again and takes a swig.

I know I owe him an apology, but I'm not sure where to begin. When did I start judging men so harshly? Was I like this before I kicked Dan out of the house? I don't think so. No, I often hung out with him and his buddies. I've always gotten along with men better than women. Except for Mum, of course, and Trix. Trix is my wildcard.

"But, you're the media. Are you dissatisfied with your work, too?"

"I think the fact that I planned this trip is telling me something, yes. My ex was never into this trip—it was all my idea. I should have clued into her disinterest sooner." His expression falls flat and grim, and my heart pangs for him. I can honestly say I know how he feels. I never realized Dan had checked out of our marriage until it was too late. I'm not ready to share these thoughts with Pete just yet, but something stirs deep inside me when I hear him talk about his ex. We're coming from a similar place, both of us unsure of what's next.

"Lately, I've realized I don't enjoy simply reading the news. I've always regretted not being out there in the trenches, so to speak."

"Would you want to report from war zones?" I'm trying to eat this big chip and salsa without any falling out of my mouth, but I'm failing miserably. Crap. I think some just landed in my cleavage. I hope he doesn't notice.

"I don't know. I'd like to find out if I'm well-suited. I've always stayed safe. Part of my upbringing, I think. But my sister's a nurse at The Children's National Medical Center Burn Unit in DC, and she tells me all the time about young patients with brutal burns, and what she did to get them healthy again. Who do I help? I don't help anyone. I just read the news."

"I wouldn't put it like that, but I know what you mean. Your sister's so unselfish to choose to work with sick children. I'd love to help the wrongly accused, or women who can't defend themselves. Pro bono work is frowned on at our firm."

"'What's in it for me?' Everyone asks that, right? It's the way of the western world. I guess I'm hoping this trip will enlighten me on other ways of thinking."

"You sound like you're going to make me climb Mount Hiei and become a Buddhist monk."

"Well, Japan isn't a stop on this trip, but never say never," he says with a grin.

"The monks of Mount Hiei walk fifty-six miles a day for one hundred straight days to attain enlightenment," I answer.

"To hell with that, let's enlighten ourselves on a rooftop terrace in Rome." Pete laughs and raises his glass my way.

"I didn't say I was joining you, yet." I smile at him and get out a pen and paper from my purse. Trix and I came up with a bunch of questions together. Okay, mostly me. Trix only wanted to know if he wore boxers or briefs.

"I have questions."

Pete grabs a chip, dips it in salsa, and bites into it. "Okay. Shoot. I'm all yours."

He talks while eating. Well, I don't think that's a deal-breaker. Besides, it's just for three weeks. Just a travel companion. Dan used to text at the table all the time. Pete's looking right at me, fully engaged.

"Why are you doing this? You're over forty. You're successful. Well-known, at least in North America. Can't you just go alone?"

He looks at me in silence for what feels like forever, but I'm sure it's more like 30 seconds. I learned a lot from cross-examining people; he's deciding how much to share.

"Actually, no. I'm... well, funny, no one else asked me this, and I wasn't prepared to talk about it... So, why am I telling you this? I don't know. It's embarrassing. My father was a salesman who traveled a lot. He left us when I was just five. I don't think I've ever recovered—although I thought all those years of pushing it under that rug was going to work.

"So," he swallows hard, "I have this fear of traveling alone. I guess it reminds me of the abandonment." He looks down at the pasta he ordered and moves it around the plate with his fork.

"But if you travel with a stranger, you'd be abandoning your own circle of people, no?"

"I guess I don't see it that way. I just don't like the feeling of sitting alone in a plane, or on a train."

"Oh, I just love that. You can get lost in your own thoughts as you look out the window..."

"And see the clouds zoom past as the plane falls tragically to the ground, yes. I love that part too." Pete chuckles, but I can tell from the expression on his face that he despises flying.

"Oh, see, now I get it. I'll be flying with a wimp! No wonder the other Allies weren't interested!" I laugh. I can't help myself. He's grinning. He takes teasing well.

"I'm not afraid of flying. I just prefer company."

"Well, maybe I'll be there to hold your hand," I tease and notice his cheeks are flushed red. Interesting. I should let up a little… Naw. He's a big boy.

"Look. I know it makes me sound weak, but, there it is."

"Well it's a lot better than what I thought vying for the ticket was all about."

"What did you think it was about?"

"Pete's Lottery to get Laid."

Pete bursts out laughing. He actually has small tears in the corners of his eyes.

"Oh, Allie, no. No, it's definitely not that. I just broke up with my girlfriend of one year. I'm not looking, either. I don't… Look, I'm not a just-sex kind of guy." He hands the waitress both our empty plates and nods at my empty beer glass.

What the hell. Yes, I'll have another.

"That was my next question. God, not about the sex. I mean, I love sex, too, but, oh, fuck it!" I'm fumbling my words like a football. I take a deep breath in, exhale, and try again. "What I mean is, are you over her?"

"Yes, it stings, but I'm okay," he replies quickly. "But why would that matter, travel mate? You brushed off my marriage proposal earlier." He winks at me.

Do I sound as conflicted as I feel? And what was that nonsense about liking sex? I love sex! But did I really need to tell him on our first meeting? Shit. Am I ever going to be any good at this? Spending time with a man again after all the heartache? Am I up for this?

Chapter Ten

I think I'm actually up for this. But I need another opinion, because, *hiccup*, beer. The beer could be making me impulsive. I need Trix. I need to call the Wambulance!

The Wambulance is our way of telling one another that we have an emotional emergency. We've used the term since our twenties. I was studying world culture theory at the time, pre-law, and one night I felt it necessary to tell Trix that the problems we whined about all day long were nothing compared to others not as fortunate—those of women in third world countries, for instance. I hate how I thought I knew everything in my twenties.

"I agree, Al, but still, I've got problems. Please, let me call the waahhh-mbulance." She laughed. "We don't need to complain to anyone else because we can always vent to each other. We've always got each other." That's how it started, and we've relied on the Wambulance to keep us strong ever since.

I stand up and excuse myself. Maybe the walk to the restroom will force the salsa resting in my boobs to fall down. It's not like I can dig it out in front of Pete.

Okay, not so sure that worked. Will have to do a look-see inside a cubicle. Damn you, big, dense breasts. You're a personality all on your own. If I put you on the stand, under oath, you'd have stories to share.

Once inside the women's restroom, I look around. No one's here, so I can probably give Trix a call. She often reads texts, but forgets to respond. She'll pick up if I make it ring.

I open the far cubicle, go inside, lock it, then shake my top. A clump of salsa falls to the floor. Did you enjoy your adventure in there, sa-sa-sa-salsa? Oh, you silly drunk girl. Should have eaten more of your sandwich with the booze.

Okay, there's Trix's number. Good. It's ringing. She picked up!

"So? So?" She sounds anxious. I knew she'd been waiting to hear.

"I think I'm going to do it," I whisper, concerned anyone coming into the restroom might think I'm talking to myself in here.

"What? It's not a great connection. Repeat that," Trix says.

"I'm going to do it."

"What?"

"I'M GOING TO DO IT!" I shout.

"Oh, Al, that's fantastic! So, you get along with him! Could there be romance in the air, too?"

"It's far too early."

"I don't think so." She giggles. "Your voice is all girly-girl. You're into him!"

"Yea, baby, that's right." I laugh. She's breaking up again. I'm not going to be able to ask her anything else. I'll have to decide this one all on my own.

"Gotta go, later," I whisper and unlock the door.

A grey-haired woman is standing against the counter, waiting for my cubicle. She's giving me the strangest look, like she's repulsed by me. Beside her, a brunette is rolling her eyes. I bend down a little to look under each stall. Pairs of feet poke out from all three. How did it fill up in here so fast?

Oh, God. I quickly replay my conversation with Trix in my mind:

"I'm going to do it. It's far too early. Yea, baby, that's right."

What did they think I was doing in there? I must have sounded absurd. I'm dying. I'm DYING!

I try to pump soap from the broken dispenser, but it takes forever, and then falls apart, the lid crashing loudly on the counter.

"Oops," I say, and rush out of there as fast as I can. Halfway to our booth, the waitress stops me abruptly, grabbing my arm.

"Excuse me," she says.

No. No! She didn't hear me in the cubicle too, did she?

"Yes?"

"Honey, look down," she whispers.

I take a look. There's a long string of toilet paper attached to my left boot. It's almost all the way back to the bathroom. Why did no one else stop me? Why?

There are two kinds of people in this world: those who tell you there's toilet paper attached to your shoe, and those who laugh about it and say nothing. I'm relieved she's the former. I thank her, bend down to rip it off, and place it in the bin by the door. Then I try to walk with what little composure I have left back to our booth.

Okay, breathe. You are calm, cool, and toilet-paper-free. Don't let on what you've decided.

I give Pete a bright smile as I sit right back against the booth's padding and lean my head on it. The waitress brings me my new pint, and I take a good, long sip through the foamy head. Pete stares at me for a moment. I wonder what he's thinking.

"Alright, Ms. James, I'm starting to feel like this is *The Allie Interviews*. You're asking all the questions. Is that truly fair?"

This beer is going down nicely. "Doesn't matter because you're the one who needs a travel companion. I could take or leave this trip," I blurt.

Pete ignores my sass, picks my phone up off the table, and smirks.

"So. You say it tells a lot about a person. May I?" He winks.

"I'll show you mine if you show me yours," I say.

I can't believe I've repeated his earlier innuendo, only, I did it on purpose. I'm flirting with him! I'm actually attracted to a man I thought was an egotistical jerk only yesterday. Turns out, he's charming, funny, thoughtful, and I have no freaking clue what is happening with my hormones. I didn't think I could ever feel interested in dating again after what Dan did to me.

I grab my phone from Pete and unlock it, and he follows suit. Ten seconds later, he's scrolling through my contacts. Maybe this wasn't my best idea. I'm drinking with a guy I just met, and he's got my phone. I may as well be stark naked.

"Okay, then, who is Trix?" he asks.

"That's my best friend. I've known her for thirty years. I'll probably have her drive me to the airport since my girls will likely want to sleep in. Teens, you know."

"This is you with your girls, I think? Nice shot. You look like sisters." He shows me the photo taken last summer of me, Kayleigh, and Emma on the beach. It turned out pretty well, but I didn't think Pete would see me in a bikini this soon. I can feel my cheeks growing hotter by the minute. I need to get the attention off of me. I start scrolling through his contacts.

"Who is Garrett?"

"He's the CEO of NBC, and he's been a buddy of mine for the last three years. He's also Irish, so, we can relate. He's cool. We golf, but he's much better at it than me."

"Conflict of interest, much?" I smile.

He shrugs his shoulders. He doesn't seem offended. "No, we keep it in check. It's not like he's cutting me my pay check. Mind you, there is that Swiss bank account we set up…" He grins.

I move to his photos and scroll through them quickly. Most of them appear to be taken at work. He's either at the news desk with a colleague, or, ha! There's one of him scarfing down a sub sandwich in his dressing room. Ew. Red onions are hanging from his lip. I'm sure he didn't want that one taken, but he could have erased it. Maybe he's not a phone person. Aw, look at this.

"Who's the furry white cat in your lap? She's adorable. I would have pegged you for a dog person. A big, strong one. Like, a Rottweiler or something."

Pete smiles. "I love dogs, but we aren't allowed them in my building. Rosa Parks is my fifteen-year-old friend."

"You named your cat Rosa Parks, as in, the celebrated black woman who refused the order to give up her seat in the colored section to a white passenger?"

"Yup, that's the one." He chuckles and looks down at his beer. "I'm a journalist. I like a good story—a story rich in history. Rosa's strength inspires me. It says that people can rise above anything."

"That is… that's something else," I say, taken aback once again by his depth. "Um, but one minor detail. Your cat, Rosa Parks, is snow white."

"Is she? I don't notice color. She's just a cat." Pete leans back. He looks relaxed.

"Oh that's deep. You, getting all philosophical about your cat." I like this guy. I can't help it, damn it. I like him. I put his phone down, and he does the same.

"White flag?" he asks.

"For now," I answer. "So, let's say I join you on this trip. What would we do in each city?"

"I didn't make a detailed plan. We won't have a lot of time in each city, so I thought we could try to be spontaneous. Explore. I haven't done that before, have you?"

"No, I've always stuck to a plan, too. I'd have to talk it over with my girls, but I think they're spending time with their dad after Christmas anyway, and they start back at school on the third. My parents can stay with them, and Trix will check in on everyone. It should work… but I need to tell you… this is the craziest thing I've done since a five a.m. Polar Bear Swim I did in high school!" I run my hands through my hair and finish the beer in my glass. "The air was freezing that day. Crazy, but not the kind of crazy that lasts three whole weeks."

I can't believe I'm going through with this! *I'm going to do it!* I chuckle at the memory of those restroom women staring at me, then sit back and catch my breath. I'm feeling drunk with anticipation, plus, pint number two is going to my head.

"I wouldn't call this crazy. We're seizing moments," Pete says. "It's good to check your own pulse once in a while. See if you're still alive."

With that, he reaches across the table and puts his hand in mine. I let him leave it there.

Pete

Heather Grace Stewart

Chapter Eleven

I drop my keys on the granite kitchen counter and rub my hands together. Brrrr. My condo is cold, as in Montreal winter cold. I was there in 2008 for a media conference and wondered what kind of messed up, self-loathing people actually live there. Penguin people.

The thermostat says it's below freezing in here. Heating must be broken. Bollocks! How can I pack or get anything else done in these frigid temperatures?

"*Mew.*"

"Aw, Rosa, have you been cold for long? Poor kitty. C'mere sweets."

I pick up Rosa Parks in one hand and grab my cell in the other. I flop down on my black leather sofa, wrap myself and Rosa in a wool throw, then dial my building's manager.

Just holding my phone—the phone she held an hour ago—makes me feel warmer.

Oh, so is this how it's going to go? I'm going to lose my head over her? This was supposed to be an uncomplicated vacation. Uncomplicated,

McCarney, you think you can do that, ever?

She's so hot, I couldn't take my eyes off her. When she was drinking the froth off her beer, it was so sexy I wanted to do her up against that old pub wall, right then, right there. The best part is, I don't think she even realizes how sexy she is. She's whip smart, feisty, damn cute when she's tipsy, and, buggerall, she doesn't want anything. She said she's still getting over her marriage ending. How am I going to keep this thing casual? How?

I give Rosa Parks a little pat and continue to hold for the manager.

I'm going to have to pretend. I'll pretend I don't like her. It's what we men have done since we were boys. Pull a girl's pigtails; stick our tongue out at her. It's simple, primeval, but it gets the job done. I'll carry her suitcase for her, but I won't do her any more favors. We'll focus on the food and the sights. I'll keep it friendly, but arms-length.

How did I throw my DO and DON'T lists out the window and wind up hugging a bloody stranger when I don't do hugs? How did I manage that one? I knew right away, that moment on the ice patch: Allie No Middle Name. I don't know how I knew. I just knew.

Well, now everything is up the shitter, and she's making me curse again. I thought I promised myself a few years back I would act more professional and cut that shite out.

"Hello," Kurt, the manager says. "If it's about the heat, we're already working on it. Sorry for the inconvenience. It could be another twenty-four hours."

"Twenty-four hours, I could be an ice sculpture by then!"

"We're advising people to stay elsewhere, at least for tonight."

"Ya think?" I'm supposed to be packing for the trip of a lifetime. Also, moping around my cozy penthouse singing cheesy Christmas carols while drinking vodka and tonics. Al's out of my life and probably not speaking to me ever again thanks to my Facebook post going viral, and Mum and Eve are too far away for me to get back for Saturday's flight. Skype and Rosa are all I've got for Christmas, but I had prepared my mind for it, and it was going to be good. A man, his cat, and Thai food from The Golden Door just down the street. Freezing my bollocks off wasn't part of the plan.

I hang up with the manager and call Garrett. He answers on the first ring.

"Hey Gar, how's she cuttin'? Look, the heating tanked in my building, and it's starting to feel like an iceberg in here..." I think I'm exaggerating, but as I look out at the city lights through my wall-to-ceiling windows, I can see frost forming on the inside bottom corners. My place is higher up, therefore, warmer. I wonder how the rest of the building is faring. I'd leave Rosa with Terry, who feeds her for me when I'm away, but his place is likely worse off than mine.

"No worries," Garrett answers almost immediately. "Come stay with us a while. You could even spend Christmas Day here, if you want."

"This is going to sound... what about Rosa Parks?"

Garrett laughs. "Pete, it's fine. We can put her with you in the back room. It's empty because Jeff is overseas for Christmas." Jeff is Garrett and Maggie's youngest son, who joined the reserves this fall.

"Well, it won't be the traditional laid-back Christmas on your sofa for me, I'll be back and forth, packing and all, but, if you're fine with that, that'd be cool. Thanks."

Staying at Garrett's isn't my ideal vision of how to spend my Christmas Eve, but his home in north Briarwood is beautiful, roomy, and he and Maggie are quite hospitable. Last night, I even managed a hot shower and hot toddy before slipping into bed with Rosa Parks at the foot.

I wanted to return to my place to pack today, but when I called the manager again this morning, he said repairs will take at least another 12 hours. They're trying to get the heat returned by Christmas Day—tomorrow—but he wouldn't guarantee it. I'm irritated with the situation and expect we'll be compensated, but I must admit, sleeping half the day today was a luxury; one I could get used to.

Garrett strides into the formal living room wearing a black shirt, matching tie, and two glasses of spiced egg nog. He hands me a glass. I feel rather dressed-down in blue jeans and my red and black rugby shirt, but I'm comfortable. I could wear this every day.

"Sorry I was at work all day, mate, some of us do have to make a living." He smirks. "How'd you sleep last night?"

"Well, the bed's comfy, but I couldn't get a wink with Rosa Parks sitting on my face."

Garrett bursts out laughing and rubs the stubble on his chin.

"That just sounds wrong, doesn't it?" I chuckle and take a sip of the egg nog. I've always hated the texture of this stuff, but I'll be polite, since I'm the guest, here.

"So," he sits down in the leather easy chair beside mine, "you've made your choice."

"I have, mind you, the ball's in her court. She hasn't texted today, but she sounded keen yesterday. I think it's on."

"There's a photo of you two circulating on Facebook, Instagram, and Twitter. She's smokin' hot. Nice going."

"She also happens to be a clever lawyer and damn funny, Garrett. I didn't pick her for her looks."

"But it has to help, her being so easy on the eyes." He grins, downs the rest of his egg nog, and places the glass on the coffee table.

"I wanted to keep her identity private. I mean, obviously she's an Allison James, but I was hoping we could leave it at that. Anyway, can you get the paparazzi to ease off? I'm sure one of your execs knows people at the tabloids ..."

Suddenly, Garrett's expression falls. It looks like he's eaten a sour lemon. He pats my forearm. "I don't think it's doing your career any harm, my friend. I'm sure you'll be fine once you two get on the plane," he adds.

"I don't think so. This has blown up bigger than I ever imagined. I'm afraid they'll follow us everywhere."

"Pete, my man, if it matters to you that much, I'll make some calls. Okay?" He gets up from his chair and starts to leave. "Stay comfy, watch some TV. I'll be back in a while."

I sit back, place my feet on the ottoman, and turn on the remote. All the comforts of home are right here. The tree in the corner is glowing with white lights and brimming with wrapped gifts beneath it. I have a warm bed and good friends to spend Christmas with tomorrow. Maggie even put out pretzels and cashew nuts, and there's a full bar in the far corner. So, why am I feeling so damn uncomfortable?

"*Mew*," says a little white fur ball at my feet, and I bend forward to pick her up.

"Rosa! You're not supposed to be out here. The deal is you stay in our room. Just until we get home, okay?" I'm talking to my cat like she's a person. I seriously need to get out more.

I get up with Rosa tucked under my left arm, walk into the hallway, and turn left toward our guest-room. We're about to pass Garrett's office on the right side. As we draw nearer, I hear shouting. It's Garrett.

"Can't you hear me? Should I call back? I said I'll cover all expenses. Just trail their every move, then send the best photos to *No Way!* and *Celeb Stalker.* You can also just post directly to our NBC News Facebook page. Oh, and get lots of the girl. She's the real money."

I lean my back against the hallway wall, close my eyes, and take a deep intake of breath to calm myself. I'll knock him out cold if I don't calm down first.

I slam the office door to keep Rosa in, put her down, and rush forward, pushing Garrett up against the wall. He still has the phone in one hand. The other one is shielding his eyes.

"This is what three years of loyal friendship and two thousand dollar golf clubs bring me? This? You've been calling the paparazzi?"

"But Pete, my man, don't you see? It's genius! Ratings for the news show, hell, ratings for the whole network, are gonna skyrocket. You can even have your own reality show when you get back."

"I don't want a shite reality show. I want my reality. I thought I was getting that with this dream trip, but you've gone and ballsed that up." I take him by his collar and push his neck farther into the wall. He's turned white, and he's sweating bullets, but he knows better than to move out of my hold. I've got at least 40 pounds and a half foot on him.

"Pete, buddy, it's a win-win! Your career will soar, and the network will be back to what it was three years ago!"

He's shaking, and, dear God in heaven, there's piss at his feet. I sigh and let go of his collar, throwing his arse into his own pool of piss.

"You're pathetic. I thought our friendship meant something. Why do people always manage to fool me like this?" I say, more to myself than to Garrett.

"Because you're naïve. Ever since your daddy left, you're looking for someone to trust again. But guess what? That's not gonna happen. The world isn't innately good. Get real!" he sputters from behind his desk, below me.

"Boys? Hello?" Maggie bounces in with an apron round her waist, a smile on her face, and a tray of hors d'oeuvres in her right hand. "Pig in a blanket, Pete?" She's completely unaware that her husband is cowering behind his desk in a puddle of his own piss.

"Thanks, Maggie, but I'm not staying." I lean in and kiss her cheek, feeling badly that I'm spoiling her Christmas Eve. It's not her fault her husband is a sneaky, back-stabbing arse.

I gather up Rosa in her cage, throw my coat on and my small duffel bag over my back, and head for the front lobby. Garrett has composed himself and rushes to stand before the front door, blocking it. Maggie is behind us, her mouth wide open, but she's still holding her tray of pigs in blankets.

"C'mon man," Garrett says. "It's nothing but a bit o' publicity. You always liked being in the limelight."

"You're wrong. You always wanted to be in the limelight. I just wanted to give people the news. But fools like you make it all about ratings, advertising, making a fast buck. I just want to share the real story."

"Yes, and you and Allie, you're the real story!" Garrett jumps as Rosa Parks hisses at him.

"We could be, if you'd get out of our fucking way, *A bhastaird mór*," I say and shove him aside so I can walk out his front door.

Oh, buggerall, it's a cold, wet snowfall outside. This is miserable! I want to turn back just to stay warm and dry, but my pride won't allow for that. I keep on walking down their slush-covered stairs, then onto the sidewalk. Don't look back. Don't look back. My hair's already soaking wet, like I've taken a shower. Rosa hisses and howls up at the velvet, starless sky, my arms wrapped around her cage like a hug.

"Shhh, Rosa, it's going to be okay."

"Come back, for God's sake, come back. It's Christmas Eve, brother!" Garrett shouts from his front steps, but his words are slightly muffled. The arse. His mouth is full of pigs in blankets.

"You are not my brother, and I'd rather be alone on Christmas than spend it with a phony like you," I shout back and nearly slip in a pile of slushy snow as I turn on my heels and walk around the corner, out of his sight.

Five minutes have passed and still not one cab in sight. I will not call for an NBC car. That's absolutely my last resort. My face is frozen, my eyes are blinded by the snow, and I can't feel my feet. Poor Rosa looks like a wet mop. Maybe if I stand under this streetlamp, I'll be able to see my phone well enough to call for a cab.

I get my phone out of my duffel bag, and within seconds the screen is covered in snow. It's not wet anymore, but it's still coming down fierce. Bollocks. I look up, hoping to find some kind of shelter. Then I see her.

"Pete? Is that you? What are you doing here?"

It's her. It's Allie. She looks like an angel, her face backlit by the orange glow of the streetlamp, tiny, frozen snowflakes adorning her long, wet hair like baby's breath.

"You're a dog person? You never told me that." She's got a black and white Border collie on a leash at her feet.

"You were a little busy telling me how much you're a cat person."

"I didn't say that. I said … never mind for now. It's cold and wet out here. I'm trying to get a cab back to the city. I guess you live nearby?"

"Yes. Why are you in Briarwood?"

"Garrett lives round the corner. The heat in my building is broken, so I was staying with him, but it turns out he's a lying son of a bitch." I won't mince words. I'll explain the rest later.

"Oh, no." She looks slightly amused. I'm not sure if it's my slick hairdo, or that I've suddenly got a potty mouth that's comparable to hers, but she definitely looks pleased to be standing here, with me, in the cold, wet, snow. Odd.

"Do you want to join us? I've got an extra room and plenty of turkey for dinner tomorrow. We'll be together for three weeks anyway—we may as well start now."

Rosa looks down at the dog and gives him a long, irate hiss. I'm sure we can separate the animals. My problem is how to deal with the humans.

Together. She said it. She's decided. That's wonderful. But, this invitation... what am I going to do? If I go to her house, I'll meet her teenage girls. Possibly, her parents. I don't know if I'm up for that. I was going to keep this arms-length. Christmas dinner can be messy. What if they have those Christmas crackers with the paper hats in them? You wear a silly paper hat with someone, and they never look at you the same way again.

I look at her, a halo of light circling her head, a smile on her face that feels like coming home, and I can't resist. I want to scoop her up and carry her wherever she wants to go.

She's not looking for love, McCarney. Calm down. You have to keep it cool. Don't mess with your heart again. Don't risk it.

"That would be nice," I say, and the dog at Allie's feet wags its tail and jumps up eagerly, sniffing Rosa through her cage. Rosa hisses once more, then turns around so she's not facing him.

"This way." Allie gestures for me to follow her. "It's about four blocks." She holds up a brown paper bag. "I had to run out to get some cranberry sauce before everything closes."

"By the way," she smiles broadly, "this is Martin Luther King. We call him King for short." She looks up at me, bracing herself for whatever repartee I wish to throw her way.

What she doesn't know is that she's left me breathless. I stay silent, watching the snowflakes dance around her hair as we saunter up the quiet, oak-lined street.

Allie

Chapter

Twelve

Christmas Day

Pete has just offered to help Dad carve the turkey. I fight the urge to run for cover. World War III might soon break out. In my Ikea kitchen.

Everyone in our family knows that Dad has turkey carving down to an exact science. Anyone interfering with his process could make the difference between eating hot turkey in the next 10 minutes and eating cold turkey two hours from now.

"You want to carve the bird?" Dad stops what he's doing and stares at Pete through his bifocals, sizing him up the way he's sized up every man I've ever brought home.

Dad's wielding a very large kitchen knife and wearing an apron that says 'Trust Me: I Know A Shortcut'. It was made before GPS existed, so only us over-40s get the joke, or maybe just my family, where the three of us would drive for an hour, taking one of Dad's "shortcuts," only to find ourselves back in the same spot an hour later.

"I can help carve the bird, if you'd like, Mr. James," Pete shouts above the clatter of Mum checking and rechecking every pot on my stove top. He looks nervous, realizing he's treading on uncharted territory. Even Dan never carved the turkey. Of course, Dan never did anything to help us out in the kitchen.

"Mr. James is my father's name. Please. Call me Dennis," Dad says, and he hands him the knife and pats him on the back. "You take over. I'll hold the plate and the light over it so you can see." I breathe a sigh of relief. Dad actually handed him the carving knife! Thank God. No one is being murdered tonight, unless I've severely misjudged Pete.

As the two of them wrestle with the turkey, Mum heats up some plates, and Trix, Kay, Em, and I put the finishing touches on the table. The girls are wearing the new long sweaters and leg-warmers I got them for their ski trip. They're anxious to spend time with Mandy and excited for me to go on my adventure, but insist that I Skype them every few days with updates and to let them vent about everything Dan & Lori.

Everyone seems to like Pete, and I was relieved when the girls insisted he stay for supper tonight. He was a little cool and grumpy near the end of the day, but I suppose Christmas with near-strangers, his heating still not fixed, and having to keep King and Rosa apart are all stressing him out. Rosa's in Pete's room in the basement, and King keeps sticking his nose under the door, barking at her. The girls find this hilarious—Rosa, not so much.

When everything's ready to be served, Pete pulls out Mum's chair for her, and she sits down, smiling up at him as he pushes her seat closer to the table.

"Thanks, Pete. I still can't get over how I don't know you from TV!" She shakes her head as she grinds some pepper on her mashed potatoes. "And everyone says I should!"

"Gran," Em says, passing her the rolls, "he does the news every night. Don't you watch that?"

"Oh no, not anymore. No, I read my papers, but the news got annoying once you had to start reading that ticker thingy at the bottom, watch, and listen all at the same time."

"You don't have to read the ticker, Gran." Kay smiles and passes her the butter. "You can ignore it."

"You girls are used to nine hundred and ninety-nine items in your line of vision. You're all about the notifications. The multimedia. One medium is enough for me. My canvas and my paints. That's all I need."

"Louise has some of her work in a small gallery up state," Dad tells Pete as they take turns pouring gravy on their meals. I can hear the pride in Dad's voice. Forty-two years, and most days, they still like one another. I wish I knew their secret.

"Don't go to bed angry and don't stop having the sex," Mum told me a few years back when I called to ask her for marital advice. I couldn't believe that was her only advice for making a marriage last, so I pressed her for more.

"It's good to make them think they're the boss, even if they aren't. Stroke their egos. Make them feel useful. That's all they want. It's their instinct to be our cave men—to provide for us and protect us. So, let them have that. Make them feel like they still rule the cave."

"Jesus, Mum! You're telling me to con my husband and butter him up?"

"Pretty much." Mum chuckled.

"I'm a successful lawyer. Are you saying stop being a successful lawyer?" I asked.

"God no. You keep doing that. You just thank him when he supports you doing that."

"I'm up and out of the house before he's even out of bed."

"Well, does he make sure King is walked and the girls get to school?"

"Yes, he does, but—" I didn't tell her that he complained every step of the way.

"So you make sure you appreciate him for that. I'm just saying, don't take each other for granted. And that leads me back to the sex…"

"Ok, Mum. That's great. Have lots of sex. Got it." I could hear Em coming swiftly into the kitchen. "Gotta go. Thanks for the help," I said before hanging up.

She may be direct and hard-headed in all that she says and does, but Mum truly has guided me in my relationships, through all stages of my life. Earlier today, she even pulled me aside for a bathroom chat.

"Door locked?" she said.

"Yup, but I'm not sure who's watching the potatoes. We can't stay here long," I said, checking my hair in the bathroom mirror. It was an unruly mess, frizzy from the heat of the oven.

"I just need to say, he's kind, and clever, and yummy!"

"Thanks, Mum, but we're not going to get involved. It's just a trip. A three-week trip."

"Uh-huh." Mum fixed the collar on my blouse, which had been lop-sided.

"No, really. He's just out of a relationship, too."

"Allie, it's been over a year. Even the girls are ready for you to…"

"Enough, Mum. Maybe I'm not ready. Maybe… I'm not." I looked down at the floor, tears welling in my eyes.

With that, she took my face gingerly in her hands, then pulled me in close for a hug. "I know, Al. I know. Guard your heart. But don't over think things, either. That's a real waste of time, and we both know how precious little time we all have."

I thought back on our last few years of tragic loss. Mum's brother Rob had battled a rare form of cancer and lost that fight two years ago. Her uncle Chris had passed away from a brain tumor, and we lost both her Mum and Dad's Mum last year. We filled their seats at the table with friends like Trix, Brad, and their daughter Melanie, and tonight, we'd added Pete, but the loved ones we lost left a gaping hole in our gatherings, and in our hearts.

A loud knock on the bathroom door startled us.

"Psst, Allie. Louise. It's Trix. Let me in!"

Both of us knew Trix didn't actually need to use the bathroom. These bathroom chats were becoming an unspoken holiday ritual for the females in our family, and it appeared we were extending membership to good friends like Trix.

Trix slipped into the room, a glass of Shiraz in hand. She's the smart one; she brings red wine to these bathroom gatherings. I must remember to do that next time. I leaned against the marble blue counter and sighed.

"I suppose you want to talk about me and Pete," I said.

"Well, duh," Trix said.

Mum chuckled.

"Brad likes him. He said he had a firm handshake, but not too firm. Apparently that's a thing that matters."

"Oh God. If you're about to ask about size next, I don't know, and I don't wanna know."

Mum and Trix burst out laughing.

"As if!" Trix retorted. "Of course you want to know!"

"My mother is standing right here." I snickered.

"Dear," Mum smiled, "it's possible I know what you're talking about. I may have had sex at least once. We had you."

"Can we get back to the cooking? I have to defrost dessert." My face was flushing red.

"And here I thought we were getting to dessert, just now." Trix chuckled and downed the rest of her wine.

Another knock at the door.

"Mum! Let us in!"

The girls pushed their way through the door, past Mum and Trix. Trix locked it, although I really didn't get why, since now more than half my dinner guests were gathered in my bathroom.

"We wanted to know what we were missing," Kayleigh said, putting down the toilet seat cover so she could sit.

"Yeah, did we miss any good stuff?" Emma started flossing her teeth over the sink. This was getting ridiculous. And hot! It was getting super hot in there.

"No girls, we were just about to head back to the kitchen," Mum said.

Good. At least some things in this family were still private. Still sacred.

"We think Pete is a glorious sex bomb and that your Mum should consider him, you know, more than a friend," Trix blurted. "How do you girls feel about him?"

"He's real nice!" Em said, not phased at all by her "Auntie" Trix's candor. "He actually helped me do some rug hooking by the tree. It was that rug hooking of three cats that you gave me. He actually got into it. I couldn't believe that." She giggled.

"He's tall," Kayleigh said, probably unaware that as she said this, she was correcting her own posture. She often hunched over, self-conscious of her 5'8" frame, beside her friends. "I bet he'd play basketball with me. I'd love that." She shifted a little on the toilet seat and looked down at her phone, checking her Twitter feed. Twitter: where you can read porn and be saved by a biblical quote, all while having tea and toast. I didn't interfere with what she did online anymore, but I had to admit, I was curious.

So, Pete had made an impression on my family. A good one. Still, I wondered what to expect from tomorrow. Would he act differently when we traveled? Would he want to do the same things I wanted to do?

Back at the table, my stomach's feeling uneasy. I pick at my chocolate pie and ice cream, barely touching it. I know that I have to let go of all these concerns and just take a leap of faith, but it isn't easy after the year I've been through.

"Okay, cracker time!" Mum announces, and the table grows loud with raucous excitement as everyone grabs one side of a Christmas cracker, makes it explode, then starts discussing their prizes and playing with them. Alternatively, some, like Brad and Trix, get a complete dud, and end up arguing over who caused the cracker to not-pop. It's beautiful chaos. On top of all this noise, King is running around the table, trying to catch any falling food. He's also chasing Rosa, who someone accidentally let out. She's swatting King with her paw and hissing furiously, either at King or the flying cracker prizes—I'm not sure which.

Pete turns to look at me with an uncertain smile.

"So. I guess you're a cracker family."

"We're a cracker family."

"I can work with that," he says, his half-smile turning upwards into a grin. He pulls the other side of my purple cracker, and it bursts open.

Something small and round comes flying out of our cracker and nearly lands in the cranberry sauce. I grab it and unwrap the plastic covering. Pete leans in to get a closer look, and we bonk heads.

"Wait, you have to wear them, you two! You're the only ones not wearing them!" Em giggles. She stands up, reaches for my hat, and pulls it down over my head. It's a brilliant yellow crown.

"Look at you, Princess, all set for Windsor castle." Pete laughs and starts fiddling with his folded purple crown. "Too bad we're only stopping in London."

Princess. I love the nickname he's just given me, but I won't tell him so.

"I can't wait for London. And you don't have to wear it," I say.

"No." He hesitates a minute and sighs, looking down at his empty plate before looking up again.

"It's fine. I think I just left the world of NBC, but I can still be King of the World. Shall I wear it for our travels?" he says, placing the paper crown on his head.

The NBC thing is news to me. Guess we have some catching up to do on the flight tomorrow. I glance at him when he's not looking my way. He even looks delicious in a silly paper hat. I try to look the other way, but now he's handing me something.

"Did you get a good look at the prize?" he asks and hands me the unwrapped cracker gift. It's a tiny blue compass.

"Perfect for when we get lost in the Marrakech desert." He grins, and I hear Mum choking a little on her wine.

"Merry Christmas, Allie." He clinks glasses with me, his sea-blue eyes looking right into me. It feels like no one else is in the room. I can't eat, I can't concentrate, and my heart is pounding in my ears. This can't be good. Did I remember to have bloodwork done this year?

"Merry Christmas, Pete," I say rather breathlessly.

Well, *fuckshitdamnitall*, and yes, I'll have whipped cream on that.

I am in so much trouble.

Chapter

Thirteen

"Okay, let's set some rules for the rest of this trip," Pete says as he unbuckles his seatbelt. We're seated in cozy Business Class pods, side by side, but with a low partition between us. He's been quiet since the moment we took off a half hour ago, and I know it's his nerves.

"Rules? I thought we were throwing out the rulebook for this trip. Going with the flow. When in Rome... do as the Romans do and all that."

Maybe I should stop making the cliché jokes. What if he's attracted to the classy-lawyer side of me? Although, he didn't mind the toilet-paper-trailing, salsa-down-my-boobs me, or the beautiful chaos that was my family at Christmas. I love how I can just be myself around him. With Dan, I was always trying to live up to who he wanted me to be. He wanted me to wear high heels to get shapely legs. He wanted me to be partner. Did I ever really want to be partner? I feel like that version of me was another woman entirely. I glance down at my feet. Ah, teal-blue, "Get There" walkers. They're the best.

A beaming flight attendant has asked Pete what he'd like for breakfast.

"Do you have any breakfast burritos? With Monterey jack cheese? And could you possibly bring me two papers? Thanks."

I order French toast and coffee. When the attendant is gone, I lean over the partition to talk to him again. I hate this partition thing. It's probably convenient for married couples who don't want anything to do with each other, but I actually want to talk to Pete.

"Pete. I took Psych 101. I know what you're doing here. Rules? Two papers? You're trying to feel like you're in control when you are absolutely, positively, not one freaking iota in control."

"Thanks for the pep talk, Allie," he says and starts to put on his headphones as the attendant brings us our food. "Really helped."

Seriously? Is he seriously shutting me out?

"Oh come on! You'll be fine, don't be a wimp." I smile up at him, and he slides the headphones off and down his neck, letting them sit on his shoulders. He attempts a smile back, but it looks forced. The plane veers a little to the left and shakes up and down. Our trays start rattling; my coffee rolls around its mug in a mini tsunami.

"It's better having you here beside me," he says over the turbulence. "So, thanks."

"I suppose if I weren't here you'd be flapping your arms and screaming every time the plane did that?"

"No, usually I remain calm and simply lead everyone seated in Business Class in the *Shake It Off* dance," he says.

"Cute, I'd like to see that." I'm cutting into my French toast, but my attention is quickly averted to someone on the TV screen in front of me. It's Pete, on the news, shoving some scrawny man in a shirt and tie up against a wall! Holy crap! What is this?

"Pete, you have to look at this." I turn up the sound on my remote. A leggy woman is now on camera, giving the news.

"Mr. McCarney has agreed to leave NBC, effective immediately, and CEO Garrett says he won't press charges. Mr. McCarney is headed to

London today, the first stop on his six-city tour with Rubicon, March & Morgan attorney, Allison James. He couldn't be reached for comment."

"*D'anam don diabhal!* What. A Load Of. Complete. Bollocks!" Pete's staring at his own screen, his jaw dropped. His face has lost its color.

"Was that a privately filmed video?" I ask, still cringing at the mention of my name and workplace. "It looks like that's a home office. And... what did you just say in Gaelic?"

Pete has his head in his both hands. He mumbles through this fingers. "I damned his soul to the devil. And yeah. The soulless shite used his own home security cameras."

"You told me what happened, and why you were so angry, but I didn't think you were... so aggressive."

"It got a little out of hand, yes. I'm sure I just rattled him. I didn't see any marks on him when I was leaving. Jesus, Allie."

A fear of flying alone is nothing compared to what I see in Pete's face now. Tears are forming in the corners of his eyes, and as the color slowly returns to his cheeks, they're becoming a heated red.

"How could he take this so far? He knows I can sue." His voice sounds more hurt than angry.

"Of course you can sue, but not for what you think. He's laying you off. He has a right to do that, Pete, he's got cause, right there on video. It isn't fair, but he has cause."

"But..." He looks confused.

I lean in so he can hear me clearly. "We can get him on libel. He can't tarnish your reputation like this. Also, we may have him on privacy. He has a right to a security camera, but you violate someone's right of privacy when that person has a reasonable expectation of privacy. I think you had that expectation, especially with the paparazzi issue and with the footage he took. We can get him."

"We? We're about to go on vacation! We were looking forward to facing great architecture and the ocean, not facing a jury."

"Hey, shit happens," I say. "And yes, we," I add emphatically. "But I can't represent you. I can get Jed or Don on it. Not Joan—I don't trust her. One of the others will rep you well. I can file it for you and get everything in motion for when we're back. It would have to wait to go to court anyway." I get out my tablet to start drafting an email to Jed.

Pete sighs. He looks somewhat relieved. "Thanks, Al. I didn't want to keep working for Garrett, or the network, anyway. But this..." He hesitates, looks down at his lap, then turns off his TV and looks at me.

"Are you sure you want to continue this?" he asks. "This was supposed to be the trip of a lifetime, but it's... it's a ballsed-up mess now."

"I'm still with you. I haven't jumped out of a perfectly good plane yet, have I?" I put my tablet on the folding tray. I can still feel my heart pounding in my ears. Is that going to stop at some point?

"You don't know where the parachutes are," he says. His brows furrow. His sea-blue eyes have darkened to grey. "Al. I'm not a violent man. This was a one-off." He nearly whispers this last part.

"I know that." I turn off my TV, too, and take his hand over the damned partition. "You weren't just angry for yourself. You were also defending me and my privacy."

He looks at me a moment. "Alright, Princess without-a-parachute, maybe you're with me, but there are millions against me," he says and pulls out his tablet. "The minute this plane lands, the media and the paparazzi are going to be all over us, everywhere we go. We need a plan of action, and sadly, it won't involve the Hilton anymore because that's the first place they'll look. They'll be chasing us."

"I'm all about the chase, 'bout the chase." I shake my booty a little in my seat, then groan loudly as I hear myself making the joke. Thankfully, though, it doesn't bomb. It's the first thing that's made Pete laugh all flight.

"Nice to hear you laughing again," I say, and he squeezes my hand for half a second, then lets it go and starts typing away on his tablet. What's with this hand-holding? I started it, despite that I said I was only looking to be friends. Am I sending mixed messages? Do friends hold hands?

Sure. Sure they do. He's going through a crisis. We felt it was needed, and we went with it. Don't read too much into it, silly girl. Damn. I could use a dose of Trix, in a bathroom with a glass of red wine. I wish she'd answer my recent texts. She only answered the one I left while waiting at the airport early this morning.

<We R off 2 London soon. Can't wait to see Big Ben!>

<Oh is that what he calls it, the cheeky monkey!>

Trix. Bless her soul. What would I do without her?

I hesitate a minute before leaping to share my next thought with Pete. Yes. He needs something to lift his spirits, and I trust him now. I should say it.

"Pete?" I lower my voice to a near-whisper. "I want to tell you now."

"Tell me what?" He looks up from his tablet. Then he sees the look on my face and remembers. "No! You're not really going to?"

He breaks into a grin before he even hears me say it.

"It's... Baldhart," I say quietly. "Allison Baldhart James."

I can't hear the pilot's announcement because Pete is laughing so damn hard.

Pete

Chapter Fourteen

"Baldhart! Sounds like we need to grab you some Rogaine!"

I'm still laughing with Allie as we walk down the gangway at Heathrow airport, but I'm conscious of people staring at us. Do they know who I am? Did they see the clip? Are they thinking I'm a violent man who had to step down from his position?

Allie gives the onlookers a once-over and, as if reading my thoughts, answers my questions. "Stop worrying about them. For one, we're in London," she says, pulling her carry-on higher up on her shoulder as we continue walking. "They never saw the clip. They were all watching football on the BBC."

"Oh, are you a Man U or Chelsea fan?" I ask, surprised she follows.

"Neither, what's the point now that Beckham's retired?" she quickly counters.

"I could use a first-rate soccer match right about now," I sigh.

"Can we get back to my second point? Baldhart is German for 'bold woman having great strength,' so, if you don't stop the teasing now, I'll beat you to a pulp with a stale pretzel."

I grin broadly, but say nothing. I love this woman's fire. My heart is pounding, and my palms are sweaty, but it's not because of the onlookers. As we head down the escalator toward the baggage area, however, it feels like my heart has stopped beating. There must be 100 paparazzi behind the roped-in area. The minute they see us, their cameras start flashing, and they start calling our names.

"Pete! Allison! Pete! Look over here!"

"Okay, bold woman having great strength, any chance you can blast your way through them and fly us to our hotel?" I shout above the racket.

"My rage might just do it," Allie fumes as she covers her face and grabs her black suitcase off the baggage turnstile. I see my large blue suitcase a little further down and walk over to retrieve it.

A few of the paparazzi have jumped the rope, and Security officers are trying to push them back, to no avail. I quickly grab Allie's hand and guide her away from the pushing, shouting mob, over to the airport's front doors.

"Try not to worry, I texted my friends from the plane. They should be out front any minute."

"You know the opening and closing airport scenes in the movie *Love, Actually*?" she says, keeping her head down.

"Yes. Brilliant film."

"This feels like the exact opposite of *Love, Actually*. More like, *Stalkers Are All Around, Actually*."

"Yeah. Love is all around, my arse." I shove one of the paparazzi out of my personal space. I seriously hope I don't get sued for protecting myself in this situation.

"I always wanted to recreate those scenes when I finally saw Heathrow airport." She sighs.

"I could plant a long wet one on you, if it'd help." We finally reach the sidewalk outside. Two more paparazzi have followed us and are shouting for us to kiss. Do they have bionic hearing as well as telephoto lenses?

"Pete McCarney!" A burly one calls to me, and I note his British accent. The others sounded American. I wonder if this is the one Garrett hired over the phone that night.

"Pete!" he continues, despite that we've turned our backs to the cameras. "Are you surprised Garrett didn't press charges? Have you been charged with assault before?"

I turn and stare at him a moment. I want to deck him. I want to smash his camera over his head.

"Don't say anything," Allie says. "I know you want to defend yourself, but don't do it. Look down, look away."

"There's Sandy anyway." I point to a white Volkswagen e-car. "This is our ride."

Allie just stands there, dumbfounded. "Electric? You're kidding, right? First, no Hilton, now, an electric car? Will we have plumbing where we're staying?"

I give her a sheepish smile and open the back door for her, because, honestly, I don't know.

Sandy gets out, gives me a nod, and opens the back hatch. He's almost as tall as me and has a similar build, but, I can't say it any other way, he's hairier. Much hairier. I'd say he was inspiration for the Broadway musical, although, that came out the year he was born, and I shudder to imagine him as a hairy baby. Gah.

My old friend has a full head of curly chestnut hair, glasses, and a long, thick beard that would make a lumberjack proud. He shakes my hand, throws our suitcases in the back, and heads back to the driver's seat. Seconds later, we're in the backseat of their car, and I'm making fast introductions.

"You're going to have to step on it," I say.

"Is there any other way in an e-car?" Sandy answers with a chuckle. "I bet you're worried we'll have to charge up halfway through. Nope. This baby lasts four hundred and fifty kilometers. We're good to go."

Allie's knees are practically up to her chin, and her eyes have grown big, but she's staying quiet. I'm sure the tiny electric car, all the hair, and Sandy's incredibly low voice have thrown her. I know she's a strong, independent woman, but if the situation was dire in there, in here it isn't looking much better.

"You okay?" I turn to look at her. Her eyes are closed, but she opens them when I speak.

"Yeah. Not the best start, that's all," she says, putting her head back on the seat and closing her eyes again.

I'm kicking myself that I didn't think to alert airport security we were coming and tell them to expect a mob. At least I thought to get Nadia and Sandy's help. They live outside of London, and Sandy knows all the side streets to avoid being trailed. I look back and notice only one car following us. Hopefully, we'll lose them soon enough.

"I'm sorry for all this. It will get better. I promise." I hope I can keep that promise.

"It's good to see you again, Sandy," I say, thinking back to our first meeting over 25 years ago. Back then, he was Alexander, but it wasn't long before I called him Sandy, just as his family did.

"Great to see you too, Nadia," I add, reaching over to her in the passenger seat. When I realize she's offering me a fist-bump, I attempt one, knowing I look like a complete fool in the process.

"Yo, Mama."

Oh, I wish I could erase saying that. I just can't pull that one off.

Nadia's just as I remembered her: petite, straight black hair down to her bum, Lennon-style shades, overalls with peace signs on them. I think she may have painted them on herself because the pattern is peeling off at the side seams.

"So, you two are on the run?" Nadia's squeaky voice is full of anticipation. Her expression says we're the best thing that's happened to her since Coachella, California, 2009.

"In a manner of speaking, yes, but we're not running from the law, sorry to disappoint, mates." I laugh. "I know you'd have enjoyed that."

I smile and turn to Allie. "I met these fine people while we were all studying agriculture at University College Dublin, or UCD, as we common folk like to call it. They were a lot more passionate, shall we say, about farming than I ever was, but I liked to tag along, and that's how I spent my first, and only, night in jail."

"You studied agriculture back in Ireland?"

I'll have to explain that one to her later.

"And you have a record? Oh Pete, this is so not good."

I study her face. She's not joking. *Damnú.* I hate disappointing her.

"We discovered a local farm was being inhumane to their pigs," Sandy explains. "They were constantly breeding them so the females were always pregnant, and they were taking the piglets away from them after just two weeks. They had their teeth clipped in half, their tails cut off, their ears mutilated, and the males had their balls ripped out—all without painkillers."

"Enough, that's enough." Allie is near tears. "That's just awful. I don't care about your record, Pete, if that's what you thought." She touches my forearm for a moment, and it sends shocks up my spine. The good kind. I pull my arm away immediately. Don't let her get any closer. Just. Don't.

"I just meant that Garrett's lawyer will find it and use it against you. I'm glad I know about it now. I'll have to send an addendum off to Jed. Continue the story."

"So. We all bonded when we were in Professor Woods' class. He was this one fab UCD professor who taught us a lot, maybe too much," Nadia says. "He told us how to get into that farm because he'd worked there as an intern years before, and he egged us on. We were young and stupid."

"Now we're just old and stupid, right babe." Sandy laughs and makes a sharp left. I look behind us. Not a car in sight and open country road for miles. That's my man.

"One spring night, we broke into the pens and stole three piglets," Sandy explains. "We had plans to take the mother too, but she nearly bit me when I tried. We couldn't lift her. All we could do was grab the piglets and run like hell."

Allie looks at me, wide-eyed. "I thought, on that first morning show interview about this trip, you said you never leapt. You never did anything out of the ordinary."

"So, I forgot about the bloody swine." I laugh.

"Where did you keep them?"

"In my dorm," I answer. "Not for long, mind you. They squealed every night. My dorm mates were sure I was having the time of my life in there. They called me a ladies' man all that week, until they heard about the swine smuggling. Then they called me Piggy for the rest of the year."

"Piggy, as in..." Allie's chuckling loudly. I prefer her like this.

"Yes, Piggy, as in, *Lord of the Flies*. It was humiliating. I would have preferred Porky."

"Let's make a deal, Piggy," she says, looking up at me, her face glowing like an angel. "You never mention my middle name again, and I won't call you Piggy."

"You've got yourself a deal, Legal Eagle."

"Hey. What happened to Princess?" she retorts quickly, but I notice her half-smile turning into a grin.

"Look. Don't get me wrong," I smile back at her, "you're gorgeous, but you're independent and tough as nails. You're no princess, and we both know it."

As she looks down at her lap, her hair falls over her eyes, but I can still see the broad smile across her face.

The drive toward Coventry is rainy, but beautiful. Lovely century-old stone homes with stunning English gardens dot the pastoral landscape. Cattle and sheep graze beside the river. At one point along the route, we spot a pair of deer prancing into the woods.

It's an idyllic vista, but the road has been zigging and zagging a good part of the way, and I'd forgotten that Sandy drives like a Formula One race car driver.

"Sandy. You want to slow her down a little so I don't mess up the back of your car?"

"Right, mates, almost there anyway!" Sandy calls from up front.

I'm keen to see the farmhouse Sandy and Nadia have built on a piece of land in Withybrook, Warwickshire. They moved to England to be closer to her parents and also because farmland was cheaper here than in Ireland. They've texted me several times about their progress since they bought the land and started building on it over a year ago. They'll be growing their own lavender on the property, and true to their hardcore ethics, they'll use no chemical fertilizers, herbicides or pesticides. The soil proved sandy and well-drained enough to grow lavender in their initial trials. This summer will be the first season they open to the public as a pick-your-own lavender farm.

Sandy and Nadia continue talking about their hopes for selling lavender while driving toward Withybrook, and Allie seems genuinely interested. Still, she hasn't had much time to digest this massive change in our vacation itinerary. I pull out my tablet from the carry-on at my feet and type a note to her, making sure only she can see it.

<This ok?> I turn the tablet so she can read my message.

She smiles and nods, then takes it and types back. <True adventure. I like Sandy & Nadia.>

I'm relieved, but I do hope I can make this up to her somehow.

Sandy pulls the car up a long, gravel driveway. There are several acres of land on either side, presumably where the lavender will be in full bloom this summer. When the car stops, we're still buckled in the back, but Sandy and Nadia jump out, stretch, and start kissing each other on their front step, despite the pouring rain.

"Welcome home, baby!" Sandy says, his low voice booming like the thunder.

"Welcome back, baby!" Nadia squeals, and still, they continue sucking face. Gah. Newlyweds, 20 years in. Amazing. I wonder if I'll ever succeed at love like they have.

It's raining heavily, so I stay and study the house from the car.

Bollocks. Now I've truly done it. This is definitely not what Allie had in mind when she signed up for this trip of a lifetime.

The log house is about the width of a camping trailer. Not the lovely modern ones with queen beds and a large bathroom. More like Barbie and Ken's 1970 camper. It's two stories, but I'm still wondering where we're all going to sleep.

"It's five hundred and four square feet, but it's five hundred and four square feet full of love!" Nadia calls out to us. "Come see! We have a green roof, and we get a break on the water bill for managing and reusing storm water!"

"Storm water? *Mother fu...* Pete! Am I getting a shower or not?" Allie looks positively pissed. She's definitely angrier than when I walked back to our interview with that leggy brunette on my arm.

"I told you they're environmentalists," I say, "but, er, did I forget to mention they're also minimalists?"

I swallow hard and don't wait for Allie's answer. I get out of that car, quick.

Chapter

Fifteen

I'm in a bad horror movie. A rotten, no good horror movie because this two-story box of a home isn't large enough to escape the wrath of Allie.

As I stare out the circular window in Sandy and Nadia's loft bedroom, I can feel Allie's eyes burning through the back of my head.

"You two can sleep up there—we'll take the pull-out wall bed down here," Sandy calls up. "It's getting dark. Why don't you take a wee rest, and we'll start a bonfire. You can use the outdoor shower, but the hot tub's already warm."

I raise my eyebrows and turn from the window to face Allie. "Bonfire? Hot tub? See? It's practically a party!"

Allie ignores me, moves to the far end of the futon, and calls down to Sandy.

"We aren't actually... together. We're not a couple." She glares at me. *Tiarna cabhrú liom.* Lord help me.

Nadia's head peeks up over the top of the loft ladder. "Oh dear. We just assumed because you were traveling all this way together..." She hands us a couple of clean white towels. Thank God she has those.

"Yes, well, I guess Pete didn't fill you in properly. And to think he used to deliver the news."

Oh, that was a low blow. Allie folds her arms and leans back against the wall, but in this small space, she's still just six feet away. Glaring at me.

"Nadia, don't you remember? This is a different Allison," Sandy calls up again.

"I know lover—we spoke to the other Allie on the phone once. They have totally different voices, and personalities. He's totally made the right choice."

This is getting worse by the minute. I try to change the subject, but then Nadia climbs down the ladder, and I hear the door slam. They've both left to tend to the fire.

"I can just sit up tonight, Al. I'll sit in the corner here against this wall, and you sleep on the futon."

She seems a little surprised, and her face softens. "The floor is practically all futon. But... okay. That would be okay, I guess." She looks tired, and not just from jet lag.

"Hey," I lower my voice to a whisper, "I'm so sorry about all this. I'm sorry about London. I truly wanted to show you Big Ben."

Suddenly, Allie is giggling. It's not just a tiny chuckle. She's covering up her mouth and trying to stop the laughter from pouring out with no luck. Good Lord, the woman has a dirty mind. I love that.

She throws her head back and releases a giant pig snort amid all the guffawing. Such a big sound coming from that tiny body! It's adorable. I want to scoop her up, throw her down on the futon, and tickle her armpits. Kiss her neck. Kiss so much more. But I can't. She doesn't want that. She doesn't want me. I'll just end up hurt and alone again.

"Hey, if you aren't quiet, they'll hear your squealing and start calling me a ladies' man again."

Allie stops snort-laughing and starts frowning at me.

"You probably planned all of this... just to get me in the sack."

"Right, Legal Eagle. Sure. You've got me. I told Garrett to publicly humiliate me. I hired hundreds of paparazzi, and I forced my friends to build a tiny house one year ago, just so I could sleep with you on a small futon in Withybrook."

"I knew it." She isn't smiling, but her eyes are sparkling again. "Case closed."

"Guys!" Nadia's calling up to us. "The rain has stopped. We've got some veggie burgers ready, and the fire's roaring."

I look at Allie as she puts her hair up in a ponytail and grabs her towel. Magic. Everything she does is magic. But, I can't complicate this for us. It's been an emotional rollercoaster as it is. This trip needs to be smooth sailing from here on out, at least until I get home, sue the pants off Garrett, and find myself a new job. It's all too much to think about. I could use a therapeutic soak in that tub. It had better be hot in there.

"Wood-fired tubs were originally a Canadian concept." Sandy takes a swig of his beer and continues answering Allie's question about the beautiful cedar tub we're soaking in.

Sandy and I are in our skivvies—his are much whiter and skivvier than mine; I'm in black boxer-briefs—and we're shirtless. It was dark enough so that the ladies couldn't see us stripping down.

The air is fresh, the stars are bright, the sky an intricate bas-relief above us. After dinner, we spotted Orion, Andromeda, and Cetus in our sky-sculpture. We reminisced about university and filled them in on our story. It's been a super visit with my crazy old pals. As for the hot tub temp, it's hot in here, alright, but not the kind of heat I'd bargained for.

Allie's resting her head back on the edge of the tub, sitting straight across from me. The moonlight shines like a low lit candle across her face. Whenever she laughs with Nadia, her breasts bob in the water like sweet, candied apples. Feckit! This is ludicrous. I can't push these thoughts away anymore. She's clever, funny, stunning, and I want her.

I think I saw Nadia loaning Allie a long, black t-shirt, longer than the one she had on today, but the thought of what she may or may not be wearing under that shirt is all I can think about at this moment. I'm also thinking about how I'd like a fourth beer, and how the four of us are getting rat-arsed. I'm not following Sandy's discourse on e-cars, tiny houses or Scandinavians. He may believe I am, but I'm not. I'm picturing Allie in pink, lace trimmed panties, and I don't want to stop thinking about that until I step out of this tub.

"Scandinavian-Canadians came up with it, I think," Nadia says. "Those clever Canucks."

"Yup," Sandy continues. "They thought of using red cedar and a wood-fired, submersed, stainless-steel fire box to create an eco-friendly tub. We just followed one of their plans and voilà."

"Well, cheers to them and to us, mates! Thanks for having us stay." I grin at my friends, and we all clink bottles and take long swigs.

"Thanks for being cool about the way we live," Sandy says. "I know it may seem a little odd, but we just got sick of all our stuff. We didn't want it to own us, so we purged."

"It's good to learn new perspectives. That's what traveling's all about. But, I need to know more about the pigs and the jail." Allie smiles. "Did you guys save the piglets?"

"Technically, we were only in jail for two hours, right?" Nadia looks at me. "That night a senior don discovered our hideaway swine in your room. Bugger. He took his job way too seriously."

"Yeah, Mum came to bail us out, but she was none too happy. I still hear about it today. When I've forgotten to call for a while, she'll call, and she always brings it up. 'Petie, I birthed ya, raised ya, and I bailed ya out of jail, and now you've gone and forgettin' your old Mum even exists?'" I grossly exaggerate her accent, but it gets a big laugh from everyone.

"I love your Mum, and you must know she loves you, too," Sandy says, wiping the sweat from his brow. "I mean, you convinced her to move to the States."

"That was more Eve than me. She wanted Mum near her when she started her work in the burns unit. But yeah… You know," I look at Allie, "I never miss Ireland until I get together with these two. Then I yearn for our youth. We were so carefree, living in the country, actually making a difference."

"So, you did save the pigs?" she asks.

"We sure did," I answer. "After our night in jail, Professor Woods helped us raise a stink at the Department of Agriculture, and they investigated that farm and shut it down."

"Those piglets are probably still living a life of luxury in some petting zoo," Nadia adds.

Those piglets are probably bacon, but I'm not about to say that. I'd be throwing myself in front of a hippie peace train. Besides, Allie is looking over at me with those adorable doe-eyes.

"Speaking of a life of luxury, why didn't you continue doing those underwear ads, Petie? You were making so much money. And that tooshie! Whew! Si-si-si-sizzlin'!" She laughs.

"Underwear ads? You went from agriculture, to underwear, to anchor? Okay, Pete. Spill. I can find out if you don't tell me, I know how to access sealed documents." Allie gives me a sly grin. Nadia's snickering.

I can feel my cheeks growing hotter by the second. Buggerall. I guess it's time to share.

"I moved to New York because Evie was studying here. I wasn't interested in agriculture—that was just because I'd been in charge of the farm... after our father left. For so many years, it was all I knew, but I wanted more. I was always fascinated with the idea of living in a big city, so, after graduation, I followed Eve to the States. I met this woman in a coffee shop who said I'd make a good model, and she gave me her number..."

"I'm sure she did." Allie chuckles.

"She was from an ad agency, okay?" I know I must be flushing red, but I hope it's hidden by the darkness and steam. I've always been embarrassed about those years, but it was great money and how I got discovered. "I did some magazine ads for a few years."

"Joe Boxer hired him!" Nadia can't contain herself. She's piss drunk and giggling up a storm. "You, my dear, need to check out old *Vogues* to get a peek o' the Full McCarney!"

Now I know the steam won't excuse the redness of my face. Bollocks. Nadia is damn funny, though, but I certainly hope Allie hasn't lost any respect for me.

"So, any news about us? Do you think they know where we are?" Allie sounds concerned again. Or maybe she's just trying to save me from any more embarrassment by changing the topic. Bless her.

"It's not a top story tonight. The Duke and Duchess had a third child, a boy. That's all the buzz in London now. Maybe the dust has settled," Nadia says. She was listening to her short-wave radio earlier tonight.

"Well, I'm shriveling up like a hairy-arsed prune," Sandy announces, and everyone laughs. He climbs out of the tub and throws a towel around his waist.

"Shall I take you to bed, love?"

Nadia hops out after him and starts toweling off. "Peace, out. My lover is taking me to bed." She giggles, twirls with her arms open to the sky, and nearly trips over a rock beside the tub. Sandy grabs her by the waist and lifts her back up to standing. "You two lovebirds can stay here as long as you like. Just turn off the burner and throw some water on the bonfire when you're through."

Allie doesn't refute Sandy's lovebird comment. She just raises her beer and bids the pair goodnight as they walk away into the house. I don't know what to make of that. I do know I can't get out of this tub just yet.

"I bet they're preparing to mob us in Rome." Allie lifts one leg up a little, enjoying the roomier tub. She's absent-mindedly playing with the neck of her beer. Now she's truly killing me, and I don't want to think about paparazzi in Rome, Prague, or on the bloody moon.

"They won't, because we have a plan, remember? We'll throw them. They won't find us, and we'll still have fun. I promise." She smiles at me, but she doesn't look convinced.

"It's starting to get chilly out, but I could last another few. Want to get out and warm up by the fire?" she asks, but she's already made up her mind. She climbs out, and I slowly get up after her, thinking I'm finally soft enough to stand up. Bollocks. Wrong. I was so, so wrong.

Allie's toweling off by the fire. She bends down to slip on her sneakers, then stands up and pulls back her hair into a ponytail. The black t-shirt she's wearing is thin and clingy. It's like her breasts have been painted black, and she's a masterpiece. Every beautiful curve and arch, each hardened nipple is not only visible, but highlighted, with the roaring bonfire behind her acting like a spotlight.

I've wrapped a towel around my briefs and made it to the bonfire, but now I need to turn away from her. I'll soon be heading down a path of no return if I don't.

"You're leaving? Shutting me out again? What are you playing me for?" she shouts as I'm walking away.

I can't handle it any more. I turn back on my heels, and in two great strides I'm in front of her.

"Me? Me playing you? You said you weren't looking for anything! Yet, you're holding my hand on the plane, laughing at my jokes, and prancing around here in a t-shirt and tiny pink panties."

"Pink panties? What the—? You're the one in your skivvies under that towel, Joe Boxer Boy!" She's laughing. She's actually laughing at me.

"Never mind." I grab her by the waist and pull her in close. Instantly, she stops laughing and looks up at me breathlessly.

"Do you want me to kiss you or not?" I ask. "Because, I'd very much like to kiss you. Right this minute."

Her mouth is on mine before I can change my mind. Her tongue flickers and tentatively touches mine, so I push through, hard, like I know she wants me to. She's moaning, grabbing at my hair, pulling me in for more, satiating a hunger. We're cold, we're wet, but our heat is uncontrollable, our connection, inevitable. Our brains formed all kinds of excuses why we couldn't or shouldn't work, but our bodies don't lie.

I sniff a strand of her wet hair as it brushes against my face and waves of desire wash through me. I want more. I want it all. My hand moves to the small of her lower back, and, losing all control, I let it slide down and under her shirt and begin caressing her ass cheeks.

Even as my towel accidentally falls to the ground, she doesn't resist. As she pulls me in tighter against her, I feel silk, soft skin, and, *Tiarna cabhrú liom*, lace trim. Grrrrr....

"You're growling." She bites my lower lip. I can tell it's on purpose.

"Yeah, bit of a growler when I'm turned on, love," I whisper.

She melts right into me and starts to kiss me where I always lose control, in that place where my neck meets my collarbone.

Suddenly, she steps and pushes me away. I can see her breath in the cold midnight air, but the fire is dying, so I can't see her eyes through the darkness.

I can hear her heavy breathing, feel her staring at me. She's a deer caught in the headlights preparing to run.

"No. No, I can't do this. I'm sorry."

And then, almost as fast as she came into my life, she's gone.

Allie

Chapter

Sixteen

What was I even thinking going on this trip? I'm not ready to be this close to a man again. This is all happening too fast.

I pull open the screen door, and I'm about to let it slam shut when I remember that I'm the guest here. I carefully close it, tiptoe in, and quietly slip past Sandy and Nadia, who are both snoring on the pull-out wall bed in the kitchen-living-room-office-bathroom.

Damnshitcrapola! They don't own much stuff, so what the hell did I just stub my toe on? I attempt to muffle my cursing and heavy breathing by hopping on one foot and massaging the other with my hands, but after four beers and all that steam, I feel dizzy and start to lose my balance.

"Woaahhh, let me help you," Pete whispers. He's right behind me, but I don't startle. I kind of knew he'd come after me.

"Uaooohgah." Sandy grunts and rolls over, but he doesn't wake. Nadia's out cold.

"I thought you'd run into the woods," Pete continues talking softly. With one arm around my waist, he guides me through the darkness toward the loft ladder.

"Yeah," I whisper. "I started to, but—mosquitoes. Turns out I'm a city girl through and through."

"Mosquitoes? Here? In winter?"

"I felt them—I swear." Didn't I?

His hand remains firm at my waist, and now I can feel his chest moving. He's chuckling, but trying to keep it to himself. We reach the ladder, and I grab the middle rung.

"Here we are. I won't sleep up there, if that's what you'd prefer, but I need to help you up, Al, okay?" he whispers, and gives me a little shove to help me crawl up the ladder. One strong hand holds my hips, the other rests at the back of my calves. If he thinks that's helping me, then he has no idea what that kiss just did to me.

I wish he'd put his towel back around his abs and cover up those wet, black briefs. He's in tremendous shape. Not that I was staring or anything—okay, maybe just a teensie weensie bit at how cut his abs are—when we were in the hot tub. When his arms were wrapped around me outside, it felt like Superman might be holding me. Superman. What the fuck am I supposed to do with that? Get myself a cape and a pair of tights and hold on for the ride?

I make it up to the loft, towel off my hair and shirt, crawl into bed, and wrap myself in the warm duvet. This t-shirt is mostly dried off, but it smells like a country bonfire. I'll take it off later, when he's not looking. Still can't believe he guessed about my pink panties. I glance over at him, standing atop the ladder, staring at me.

"Jesus, Pete, you're shivering! Here, take this," I whisper and hand him the orange blanket lying at the foot of the bed. "You've got pajamas in your suitcase right?"

"Yeah, but there was no space for it up here. It's still in the car." He sits down on the end of the mattress, the blanket wrapped tight around him.

"Look. About the kiss. I didn't mean..."

"Hey, let's just pretend it never happened," I say and immediately regret how I've said it. I can't see his expression in the darkness, but he falls silent for half a minute.

"Right," he finally says. "It was nothing. I'm going to sleep in the car." He gets up to leave.

"Wait, don't be stupid. It's cold out there, and you're in wet briefs and a blanket. I'll turn away, you take them off, wrap yourself in the blanket, and get under this duvet."

"You sure?"

"Yup. We're mature adults. It's fine," I say as he turns around.

What the hell am I even saying? I can't rest with him lying naked beside me! How am I going to get any sleep?

He turns back around, slowly opens the duvet and climbs inside, his blanket still wrapped around his body. There. He's lying down, his back to me, his head resting on the other pillow. This will be fine, then.

This is not fine! I can hear his every breath, and I think the top of his foot just touched mine. The top of his feet are extremely soft for a man. I need to stifle a moan. Oh, God. I love it. Does he get pedicures?

Now I'm thinking about the kiss. God, that kiss. He knows what he's doing when he kisses a woman. I felt weak in the knees, transported to another time and place. When our tongues touched, and he grabbed my ass, I just wanted him to carry me up here and… and now we're up here. Now we're up here, but I pushed him away. Why the hell did I do that?

Dan. That's why. I thought about Dan at the end of our kiss. I could see him kissing Lori on his desk, his hands at her waist, her skirt hiked up to her hips. His lips on her lips. Her unremorseful expression. His lies.

I can't handle this alone anymore. I need Trix. I reach for my cell, which I left on the floor beside the duvet, and check the time. 1:11. Gotta make a wish, *I fucking wish I'll reach Trix.* Okay, now I can message her. She's six hours earlier. She'll be awake.

<What does it mean that I thought about D when P kissed me?>
One minute. Two minutes. C'mon Trix, I need you.
<P kissed you? WTF?! Deets!>
<OMG, so hot. By a bonfire. Really like him. Don't want to.>
<BC?>
<Because men hurt me.>

<Shut up. One man hurt you. Get over it.> <Hit send too fast... didn't mean he isnt absolute asshole and she isnt man-stealing whore but u cant let them wreck your life. One life to live baby!>

<K. Thanks sweetie.>

<BTW Garrett guy is douchebag & u r on cover OMG magazine>

<good angle or fat one?>

<love all your angles sex bomb now go to bed. Sounds like u will need ur energy!>

<Stop it! Oh, BTW, u wanted 2 know. He wears boxer-briefs. Night.>

I grin, turn off my phone, shove it under my pillow, and sigh. Love that lady. Just love her. Maybe now I can finally sleep.

Except, now I'm thinking about my girls. I miss them. I hope they're having a good time on their ski trip. Wait. Fun, but not too much fun, because then they might start replacing me with the man-stealing whore. Would they do that? They wouldn't do that. Our bond is strong.

Damnit. I need wifi. They're in a small cabin with sketchy wifi, but I'm in a minimalist cabin, with no wifi. I absolutely need to Skype my girls. Tomorrow. Pete will help me reach them tomorrow. He'll help me. He always does...

Dear Lord, help me, the man is butt naked beside me, he kisses like no one's ever kissed me before, and he smells so fucking good.

I stare up at the cedar ceiling and count the marks on one rafter. One, two, three, four... Mmmmmm. Like sandalwood and salty sea air. Like coming home.

Gurgle Brrp Gurgle Brrp. It's my underwater ring tone. Well, at least it's not an asshole calling. But, it is my office, and it's my least favorite person there. That's the ring tone I programmed for Joan.

Nothing like being woken by the person who sent you on a forced vacation while you're on that vacation. What time is it? I reach for my phone and check. Five in the freaking morning. Ugh. I might be up before the goddamn British roosters. Can I get a prize for that?

"Joan. Isn't it midnight there? What's going on?"

"Yes, it's late for me, and early for you, but we know you're booked to fly to Prague tomorrow, and this is urgent…"

"Wait, excuse me, how would you know that?"

"Oh, one of those papers printed your flights for the rest of your trip. You know, the tabloids. You and your boyfriend are the story of the week. I've been wondering if you'll ever come back to us, or if you'll just be riding off into the sunset with him like in one of those Harlequin romances…"

I bolt up in bed, pulling the duvet and half the orange blanket close to my chest, forgetting that Pete is right beside me.

"Woah, Nellie! I'm naked here! I'm naked here!" he shouts, chuckling loudly. He scrambles for a second, but manages to quickly cover everything up with his side of the blanket. I blink and vaguely remember spooning. Yes, there was definite sleep-spooning.

If it's sleep-spooning, does it even count? I glance at him. He doesn't seem the least bit embarrassed. He's rubbing the sleep from his eyes and yawning. Okay. This does not look like a man who felt my pink-pantied vajayjay on his beautiful buttocks. Phew.

"Allie? Are you there?" Joan shouts.

I'm sleepy and scatterbrained. This is not the impression I want to leave Joan, even if she was completely wrong about the dancing elves.

"Yeah, I'm still here. What's going on, Joan? It's late there, and it's still the holidays! You're scaring me."

"Jed gave me the McCarney case. It's big, Allie. Career-altering. But, he only wants me to work on it… if you and I work on it… together."

I gasp, nearly dropping my phone and the duvet I'm pressing to my chest.

"I admit, I was a little… hasty in forcing you to take time off. Everything is chaos in this office. No one's even planned our New Year's Eve party for Thursday. You always did that.

"We want you here. We need you here. When can you get back?"

Pete

Chapter

Seventeen

"SHHHHHHHHHHHHHHUSH!"

That's the third person who has shushed us in the last 30 minutes, and we've been keeping our voices low. I was prepared for this library to be old and stuffy, after all it was founded in 1841, but I didn't expect to feel like I was back in my school uniform, risking detention. Mind you, Sandy's deep whisper sounds like James Earl Jones. Darth Vader in this library? He's not about to go unnoticed.

Allie and I are meandering through a labyrinth of book stacks containing volumes dating from the 16th century to today. She said she wanted to talk to me alone for a few minutes, so we decided to wander through the stacks without any aim in mind—that, we agreed while talking in the back of the car coming up here, is what makes libraries magical.

Allie was unusually quiet after the call that woke her up. She had what she said was a "fucking freezing" outdoor shower, and then was quiet all through breakfast. I racked my brain for some way to cheer her up, knowing something critical happened during that phone call, but that the thought of leaving Nadia and Sandy so soon was also bringing her down. I had never seen her like this, and frankly, she was bordering on depressing. Her eyes lit up the moment I suggested we tour The London Library.

"Oh! I've dreamed of going there! I adore libraries. Walking through the stacks of a library feels like walking through a silent forest in winter. I used to spend hours in the law library. The stacks reminded me of rows and rows of old oak trees. It was so exciting to discover an author I'd never heard of before. Like spotting a new bird, or butterfly."

I adore it when she's so excited about a subject and rambles on and starts talking with her hands. This time, she nearly hit my chest with her hand, she was so animated. Hearing her open up to me like that made me want to kick Nadia and Sandy out of the car that instant. Boom, like Beckham. God knows I love them, but I can't wait to be alone with her again.

"Once I'd saved enough money from the modeling..."

"Those undies people had you covered, huh," she interrupted, giggling.

"Yes, well," I said, flushing a little. "I decided to go back to school and got into NYU's graduate journalism program. That library at NYU is to die for..."

"NYU!" She practically hit me in the face with her left hand and was bouncing up and down like a teenager in her seat. "I went to law school there! I can't believe we both went to NYU and didn't know it! What year! Were we there at the same time?"

"I thought you'd read my bio... I mean geesh Al, you agreed to go on a trip with me—didn't you do your research?" I laughed.

"Oh, written bios bore me," she said. "So much stuff is completely made up on the internet. I felt I got all I needed to know about you from your phone, in that pub." She grinned. "Stop dodging the question, McCarney. When did you graduate?"

I sighed. I didn't want to find out that I just missed her. I didn't want to know. "2003."

"Oh, wow." She gasped and swept three loose strands of hair off her forehead I'd been wanting to touch forever. "I graduated from law school in 2005, then started articling at my firm. We overlapped for a year!"

Bam. Straight to the heart. I felt gutted and was relieved to be sitting down. One single piece of information had made me feel dizzy with might-have-beens. She fell silent, too and looked down at her lap.

"Well, I was married then, so…"

"We could have had coffee, though."

"Yup. Could have had coffee." She kept looking down, brushing some lint off her skirt.

I tried not to think about it, but for the rest of the car ride to London, I couldn't help imagining having coffee with her in my favorite lively spot near campus. Would my life be different today if we'd met all those years ago? Would we still be right here, right now?

Inevitable. The rest of the way to London, that's the word my heart and mind kept repeating over and over to the beat of the London Symphony orchestra performing *Pachelbel Canon in D*. Mind, my heart isn't especially attuned to the classics; Sandy had simply turned it on full-blast.

As *Pachelbel* played, we stayed alone with our thoughts, zigging and zagging in a tiny e-car all the way to London. I kept stealing glances her way.

Was she feeling it, too? Please, let her be feeling it too.

"SHHHH!"

Sandy and Nadia are giggling across the vast main room of the library, but for some reason, the librarian glares up at me and Allie. The two scoundrels have conveniently disappeared from view.

129

The view from up on this narrow iron stairwell takes my breath away. Rows and rows of knowledge line the hundreds of bookshelves above and below us. An enormous square skylight at the center of the room brings in low light and adds architectural interest. I could study these walls, columns, stairwells, and stacks for hours.

Sandy and Nadia agreed to meet us in the Reading Room in 15 minutes, where we'll be using their computers and wifi to change our departure time to a later flight, so we can throw off the paparazzi. Also, we'll get into the finer details of the case with Rubicon, March & Morgan. Allie told me we could do most of this using her phone, but I balked. I can't make major decisions staring at a screen the size of half a sandwich. And how are my big thumbs supposed to fit on those bloody small keys? Gah.

We'll have to wait to Skype our families for when we're finally in a hotel room. Rooms. Why did I say room? Damnit McCarney—arm's length. She made that very clear. Still, my mind keeps playing this lovely, vague memory of her spooning me as the early morning light fell upon our faces. Did that actually happen, or was it just a hopeful dream?

"We've spent half this trip hiding from paparazzi and the other half whispering. When are we going to start having some *fun*?" Allie mutters, looking down at her sleek black sneakers. I love that she's wearing them with that jean skirt. It's sexy, yet practical.

"I thought we did a pretty good job of that beside the bonfire." As I say it, I can't believe how I'm pushing my luck. She wanted to pretend the kiss never happened. I don't ever want to forget.

Allie ignores my comment, but looks up at me with that wide left eye and half-smile I love, while leaning against the iron railing behind her. I take her elbow and gently pull her away from the railing, and she smiles.

"Not heights, too?"

"No, not heights too, Al. I'm a one-phobia man."

She chuckles and grabs a dusty old tome from the shelf to her right. At least we're building a solid friendship, here. I suppose it's best we do forget how that kiss felt and move on. She's being more level-headed about this than I am. Our lives are too complicated right now to add romance to the mix. Hell, I don't even have a job when I get back to

New York, and it sounds like hers is rather precarious. Still, I want to know more about her—so much more. I'd like to ask her more about her ex. I wonder what happened there. She's been so secretive about it. Is he the one who's making her run?

"I just think it looks rather rickety. Be careful."

"Pete. I need to tell you more about the phone call I got this morning," she whispers.

"Hmm. Maybe we should go walk around the Square so we don't have to whisper."

Allie nods and returns her book to the shelf. It's a gorgeous sunny day, but the forecast high today was just above freezing, so we zip up our jackets, carefully climb down the iron staircase, and head outside.

Though very little is in bloom, St. James Square is still rather breathtaking in December. The old buildings along this street boast Georgian and Neo-Georgian architectural elements, and there's a large park in the center lined with gardens and mossy old oak trees. We cross the street, follow the pathway in the park, and stop in front of an equestrian statue of William III.

"There you go. Erected in 1808. Allie, we're finally seeing old London."

"It's nice, but it's not exactly Big Ben." She looks up at me. I can't read her expression.

"I'll make that up to you, somehow, I promise," I say.

She clams up for half a minute, looks away from me, and focuses her attention on a cyclist coming our way instead.

She starts walking along the path again, so I follow beside her.

"Pete. Garrett's seen the suit we filed, and he's retaliating. He told Joan he's about to press charges for assault causing bodily harm."

I stop walking. "*Cac ar oineach*, first he peed his pants, now he's crying to his Mommy?"

"Cac o what?" She walks over to a tree and sits beneath it.

I stay standing. I'm looking for something to punch. Instead, I kick the bottom of the tree with my toe. Doesn't do a damn thing for me. I could really use a golf club to throw. "It's Gaelic for scumbag. It means he's shitting on my honor."

Allie throws her head back and lets out a hearty laugh. "I never knew Gaelic cursing could be so beautiful. So precise. I may have to stop saying Mother fucker and become more cultured."

I sit down beside her and try to slow my rapid breathing. "I barely touched him, Al. I pushed him against the wall, but that was all."

"I believe you," she says firmly. "His lawyer sent the doctor's report, claiming injuries to his neck. It doesn't fit. I'll dig deeper, I promise."

"Like I said, I just held him up against the wall, and he didn't seem hurt when I left." I take a deep breath. "Can we go over where we stand? Do I need to go back to New York immediately?"

"No. The media may be all over it, but legally, these things take time. Jed investigated your case, and based on the newscast made about you, he said he could file a case of defamation on top of the other one he already filed for harassment. Those two cases could make Garrett drop his charges entirely—especially if we find what's really going on with his neck. It could be an old injury."

"That sounds like something the old weasel would do."

"He sent the paparazzi our way," she continues. "He's probably still sending them. You heard him, and Joan found even more proof of that. But Pete, this whole process could take a year, a year and a half, maybe even three years before anything even gets to trial. He may not settle, so we have to be prepared for that. You sure you want to go through with this?"

"It's the principle of the thing, Al." I run my fingers though my hair and take a deep breath. "I want people to know I'm not a violent man. I need people to know he sicced the paparazzi on us. We're victims here."

"So, this is what we do." She slaps her hand on her thigh. I love her passion. "We force him to drop his case by agreeing to a settlement in ours, but we insist on an on-air apology for broadcasting false statements about you. We'll also dangle the proof we have that he sicced the paparazzi on you. He won't want that to go public. He'll fold."

"An on-air apology for the defamation, huh. No mention of calling the paparazzi? It doesn't seem like enough. It doesn't seem fair." I frown.

"No, it never is, but at least you'll be able to work in New York again. You'll win back the respect you deserve."

"You're so damn clever at this. You truly seem to be in your element." I hesitate, then add, "Do you want to just go back? Maybe I should be there now."

"No, in fact, you should probably stay away from the city until the initial buzz about this dies down. You can sign everything from here, and I can work with Joan on the case the next few evenings from our hotel. Just research. It's fine.

"But, Pete, if he doesn't settle, Joan will be repping you. It's going to be a long, drawn-out trial, and I'm not sure you want that when you don't even have a job to come home to."

"So then, let's hope he settles," I say, take another deep breath, and exhale. She's got my back. This is going to be fine. She's going over our next steps and using a thousand legal terms: defamation, mediation agreement, settlement. All I want to do is push her against that old oak tree and kiss her, harder than I did before.

"There's more," she says.

I shake my head. It's already full of legal terms. Does there have to be more? Can't I just kiss her adorable face and make her shut up?

"Joan asked me back. She wants me back in the office asap."

My heart skips a beat. No.

"You... you want to go back? I thought she forced you to take time off until mid-January."

"No, I've already decided. I don't want to go back." Her eyes are sparkling again. "Not yet, anyway. I want this trip. The paparazzi have nearly ruined it—my ungrateful law firm isn't going to mess it up for us too. Besides, I've hardly seen anything yet."

I want to make a joke about holding her by a bonfire in my skivvies, but I bite my tongue. It's still too early to joke about that.

"You can thank Trix. She kinda helped me decide," she adds.

I wish Trix were nearby. I'd sweep her up and kiss her, then firmly shake Brad's hand.

"I like her. I owe her one, once we're back. Okay then, Legal Eagle. Let's go see Prague and spend New Year's Eve together in Rome. We'll see how you and I both feel about Bangkok, Marrakech, and Cusco then. We don't have to..."

She interrupts before I finish. "Are you kidding? Cancel Bangkok? I cannot wait for Bangkok. Give me my authentic Thai food! Give me the cities I signed up for!" She gets up, brushing blades of grass off her skirt, and takes my hand to pull me up beside her. God, she's spunky.

"Okay, let's go send what we need to the firm, and then let's get something to eat before our flight."

"Did you buy that guide book I showed you in the airport?" I ask as we make our way together up the path. "I'd like to see if there are any good Irish pubs in London. Or maybe we can find a payphone and look for one in the phonebook."

She smirks and rolls her eyes, opens her small backpack and pulls out her cell phone.

"This, McCarney, is called an app. Welcome to the twenty-first century. Where do you want to eat?"

I laugh, give her a playful shove, and grab her phone. "Just for that, I'm checking out all your photos again. Especially that one in the string bikini."

Sandy's in high form. He's standing on the wooden bench at our pub table, his glass raised high above his head. "And now, one final joke, for the road... er, for the skies, for the skies, my good friends, for the skies." He chuckles, and we all raise our glasses along with him.

Good thing Nadia's only drinking lemon water, and we're in the airport, so we can just walk to the security check within the hour. We roamed the Square some more before heading here, and even got in a little shopping. Allie picked up a beer stein commemorating Will and Kate's wedding, which had her squealing in delight. Adorable.

"So. One night," Sandy says, "Mrs. McCurdy answers the door to see her husband's best friend, Paddy, standing on the doorstep. 'Hello Paddy, but where is my husband?'" Sandy's damned good at doing high-pitched female accents, despite his low voice. It's somewhat scary, like he's been practicing in a mirror every day. "'He went with you to the beer factory.' Paddy shook his head. 'Ah, m'dear Mrs. McCurdy, there was a terrible accident at the beer factory—your husband fell into a vat of Guinness stout and drowned!' Mrs. McCurdy starts crying. 'Oh, don't tell me that! Did he at least go quickly?'" Paddy shakes his head. "'Not really. He got out three times to pee!'"

We all laugh as Sandy grins and takes another swig of his Guinness.

Nadia grabs her husband by one leg, gives him a pat on his behind, and forces him to sit. "Very funny," she says. "I'm afraid I may be in for the same kind of night with you!"

"Why don't we just say our goodbyes here." I look over at Nadia and put two twenty-pound notes on the table. She's already crying. Sandy puts his arm around her.

"C'mon, guys. You both know I'm not into long, drawn out goodbyes and emotional scenes." I swallow hard. I offer Nadia my hand, but Allie gets up and shoves it away.

"You're kidding, right, McCarney? These lovely scoundrels stowed us away from the paparazzi. They're our heroes! We're giving them a proper, emotional, *Love, Actually* farewell."

"Alright, alright." I laugh as we walk out of the pub, dragging our suitcases behind us. "Right before security, for all to see? It might bring out the paps."

"Bring 'em on," she says, putting her arms around Nadia as we reach the security gate. The two hug for what seems like forever.

"Aw, what the hell," I say and pull Sandy in for a hug. "Thanks, mates," I say, reaching out to hug Nadia. I give her a kiss on both cheeks as Al hugs Sandy.

"We won't forget this."

"You won't be able to. Look what I have." Allie smirks and hands me her phone. I'd forgotten that she took a selfie of the four of us in the hot tub. We're all grinning and holding up beers. Allie's in that sexy black t-shirt. My arms are loosely wrapped around both her and Nadia, with Sandy sticking out his tongue at the far end of the shot.

"You two sure make a nice couple. Allie, you are so much sweeter than that other Allison," Sandy says.

Nadia gives him a whack on the arm, but then adds with a wink, "We hope you work it out. We'll make you a lavender cake for the wedding."

Allie

Chapter
Eighteen

Prague
December 29

"Show me more of what that fancy phone of yours does." Pete grins, sits back, and props his feet up on the white leather ottoman in my hotel room. "Can it make Garrett apologize on-air and drop his charges? Is there an app for that?"

"Stop it, I'm not addicted to it like you're insinuating." I laugh, throw him the phone so he can check out the Foodspotting app, and return to the bathroom mirror to put on my gold hoop earrings. "I was just looking for somewhere good for us to eat," I call out to him. "Do you want to be eating in a darkened Prague alleyway from out of a trash can with the rest of the strays?"

"Hold on a second. I may be single, but you needn't call me a stray," he calls back.

"Now that we've both had proper showers, at least we don't smell like strays anymore." Laughing, I turn off the bathroom light and walk out to show Pete my 'dinner out in Prague' look. I'm feeling so fresh and alive right now. I do a little twirl, like a model on the runway, grabbing my black clutch purse off the small desk against the wall and posing with it against my hip. "Ready?"

Pete puts the phone down on his thigh and stares at me a moment. His eyes move from my black wedge heels all the way up to my tight blue jeans and crisp white blouse, then stop to meet my eyes.

"Wow. You know, we could just order in..." He laughs, and I chuckle with him, shaking my head 'no.'

This is nice. We're past that awkward stage surrounding our kiss, and now we're just going to move forward and see some of the coolest cities in the world together. Sure, we both know there's an attraction, but we don't have to do anything about that. There are some things you're just meant to ignore. It's not like I've been eyeing the door adjoining our rooms, wondering 'what if?' What if he opened that door late at night and slipped into my bed, whispering in my ear, "Can I join you, love?"

Okay, so in all honesty I've been thinking about that since the minute I saw our rooms had that door between them. But, thankfully, I got sidetracked when we got busy unpacking, taking showers, and trying to decide where we want to eat.

As much as I enjoyed our adventures with Two Scoundrels—our new nickname for Sandy and Nadia—in Withybrook, taking a shower when I first arrived in my hotel room was absolute heaven. The paparazzi miraculously left us alone at both airports, thanks to Pete's clever plan to take a later flight, and we're staying at a different hotel than the one he originally booked to throw them off further. So far, so good. No word back yet from Joan regarding the mediation agreement I drafted on my flight here, and no reaction to the email I sent telling her: "I'm taking my full vacation as per our original agreement," but that I could "still help with the case, research only, as anything else would be a conflict of interest, and I expect to be paid time and a half for this mobile work arrangement." I think she's at a loss for words.

It's been an A-plus day. I felt so empowered sending Joan that email, and then to top it off, we set foot in this five-star hotel in the heart of the old-city.

"Told you I'd make it up to you." Pete grinned as I stood gaping at the grand Hilton lobby. I was practically making out with the white marble walls.

Pete white-knuckling it through the 1.5-hour turbulent flight to Prague was a rather low point, but we got through it. Barely. I had to order him two vodka and tonics and four different newspapers to keep his mind occupied. The latter wasn't such a wise idea, because it turns out we made the entertainment headline in three of those and the business section of the fourth.

NBC Anchorman Roughs Up His Boss, Steps Down Next Day was by far the worst headline. Pete ordered himself a drink when he caught sight of that. "Bollocks! I did not quit! I wouldn't want to work for that little lying shite anyway!" he muttered.

I wanted to take his hand and tell him everything was going to be alright, but I didn't want to send mixed messages. Instead, I showed him the documents I was sending the firm and reminded him that we have a solid case against Garrett for harassment. I also told him about how I'm waiting on a second opinion from another doctor to confirm the neck injury is consistent with the events that took place Christmas Eve.

"Do you know how to not-work, Legal Eagle?" He smirked and gently closed my laptop.

"Not-work? Is that even a thing?" I laughed. "Hey, if you don't want my help... you'd rock an orange pantsuit." I smiled and opened my laptop again. I want to finish this so I can enjoy our first evening together in Prague.

"I do. I appreciate it, Al. We're going to get the bugger?"

"So bad he's going to pee his pants and cry for his Mommy," I replied.

"Am I allowed to say va-va-va-Voom?" Pete says as he stands up. He's looking gorgeous himself, dressed in Levis and a dark blue shirt that brings out his eyes.

"You're allowed, but the language police might slap you with an antiquity ticket."

"Listen, doll-face, take your fancy phone and let's split this joint." He badly mimics a gangster.

"If you keep talking like that, you're going to land in jail—and not for bodily harm. I'll just put you in there." I laugh.

I take my phone from Pete and scroll through my Foodspotting app. I was checking it out earlier. I think I know the perfect place for tonight.

Facetime from EmKay Facetime from EmKay flashes on my cell screen and my phone starts vibrating in my hand.

"It's my girls. Sorry, I need to get this." I sit down on the edge of the bed, and Pete sits back down in the white leather chair in the corner. He gives me a look and gestures with his head over to the door.

"No, no, it's fine, stay," I say as I pick up the vid call.

"Mum! Mum, it's so good to see you!" I tear up as I see Kayleigh and Emma's faces on my cell phone. It's only been a few days, but I've missed them so much.

"Hey! You finally have service at the cabin?" I ask.

"No, Mum, we're back home. Grandma and Grandpa are here with us. Dad's just leaving."

"What? I thought you were staying the week!"

"No, no. We… we weren't comfortable after all. They were all kissy-kissy in front of us," Em says. "It was gross."

"Are you freaking kidding me?" I slap my hand down on the bed. "Would he just grow up and be a father for once?

"I'm right here, Allison. I heard that." Dan's face appears behind the girls' shoulders. I don't hate much in this world, but I think I actually hate that face.

"Good. I wanted you to hear that. What were you thinking?"

"We're a couple, Al. We're maybe even getting married."

"Why are you telling me this?" I can hardly breathe.

"Because, we made a mistake, but it's done now. Don't we deserve a carefree life? Lori and I want to travel, like you're traveling now. If all goes well, I may even retire early. Can we not be happy?"

"Sure, Dan." I swallow hard. "Be happy. Just don't make out in front of our kids." I want to ask him how they're going to retire early on one salary, since she lost her license, and he owes me child support until the girls are 21, but I bite my tongue. I'll let him live in la-la land a while longer.

"Fine. I'll try to remember that next time," he says, and walks out of view.

"If there is a next time," I mutter. "Are you two okay?" I wipe a few tears from my left cheek.

"We've got them, honey." It's Mum. I can hear Dad saying the same thing in the background.

"We're good," Em says. "Trix, Brad, and Mel are coming over for New Year's Eve. We're playing charades. It's going to be awesome."

"What about you, Mum?" Kayleigh asks. "The papers say Pete punched a guy. Are you safe with him?"

I cough and look over at Pete. His cheeks are red, and he's frowning.

"He didn't punch him. It's a huge misunderstanding. My firm's representing him. We're going to help him out of this mess. And I promise you, I'm safe."

"Okay." She smiles, then adds, "Are you guys, like, going out?"

Pete's cheeks are still flushed, but now he's chuckling.

"Like I said, don't believe everything you read, dear." I smile over at him, then look back and blow my girls kisses. "I'll be home soon, okay? Let's vid again on New Year's Eve. I have to go for supper now. Love you." We wave, and they hang up.

I turn and catch Pete's eyes. He looks more uncomfortable than when Kay asked if we were a couple. I know he was expecting me to stay two more weeks, but I miss my girls. I don't know if I can last that long.

"Sorry about that," I say and put my phone down on the bed.

Pete stands up and walks toward me. "No worries about the call, but, are you okay about your girls? Their change of plans?"

"My parents are home with them. It's fine." I take a deep breath. "So, now you've met my ex," I say. "He sure knows how to make my mood go from a ten to a two in three seconds flat." I sigh heavily and flop down backwards on the white bedspread. The ceiling has an elaborate flower pattern on it. Pete sits down beside me.

"He seems like a real piece of work. But then, my ex was interesting, too."

He's never said a word about her before. I sit up and look at him.

"You two didn't see eye to eye, either?"

"Not on much, no. I often wonder what I saw in her. She didn't get me." He takes a strand of hair that's fallen over my eye and tucks it behind my ear for me. "Not like you." When he looks at me, I feel something stirring deep inside. I purposefully look down at my lap. When I glance back up, he's still staring at me. God. We'd better get up. I'm about to give in to this completely.

Would that be so wrong? I really like him. My whole family likes him. What's my freaking problem?

I know exactly what my problem is. I haven't been with anyone since Dan, and the last time we were together was... when was that? Over three years ago. I'm completely out of practice. I'd make a fool of myself. My whole body feels hot and sweaty just thinking about it. *Shitdamncrapola*. I wipe my forehead and find a few beads of sweat on my hand. Am I actually perspiring over this man?

"I'm hungry," I say. "Let's go eat." I start to get up, but Pete takes my hand.

"You're upset. I have an idea for a game that might cheer you up."

Holy fuck. He's into kinky sex games.

Chapter Nineteen

"So. Are you ready for the rules?" Pete asks me, and I grin as I look up at him. This is going to be fun.

"I am so ready. Bring it on, McCarney."

The cool air coming through the rotating glass door in the hotel lobby is refreshing, and I'm perspiring less. We're standing at the Maître D's desk near the front entrance, waiting on his answer to our question.

I was relieved when Pete's game turned out to be a touring game, and not something involving a pair of dice and me being handcuffed to the bed. Not that I'm not open to handcuffs. I just need a little time.

Wait. Did I just tell myself that I'm open to handcuffs in time? I do not recognize myself anymore. I badly need a drink. Preferably, I'll have some warm food in my belly first. Not eating all afternoon might be making me slightly loopy.

"Here you go." The Maître D hands us an envelope.

"Okay, here we have a suggestion from the Maître D for an outing tomorrow—one that he thinks will let us take in lots of sights and be memorable for us, given that we're only in Prague a short time. We'll open this up after we've completed our first two outings."

"You told him we both like the outdoors?" I plunk myself down on the white leather couch beside the desk. There's a roaring fire in the ivory, marble fireplace beside me, and this couch is so comfortable, I'm not sure I'm going to be able to get up.

"Yup, and that we want a bit of adventure." He sits down beside me, leaning back into the sofa.

"Okay, so we're supposed to do exactly what he suggests." I look at the envelope and try to push thoughts of *The Bachelor's* fantasy suite out of my mind, but I can't. I snort-laugh a little, and Pete gives me a half-smile. I love how out of touch with pop culture he is at times. It's endearing, given that he was a news anchor. I really don't think he was well suited to that job. He's too clever for it.

"What? What's so funny? That's how the game works. We have to take a stranger's suggestion for tomorrow's outing, but tonight, I decide where we eat, and tomorrow, you decide where we grab breakfast. Sound good?"

"Sure, sounds good for you, because I have this Food app. I'm bound to find something perfectly suited to your tastes. What are you going to do? Wander into the first place that doesn't have blood on its windows and spiders hanging over the door?"

"Actually, that sounds appealing to me. I thought we were trying to be adventurous here." He looks at me a moment. "I do have a phone, Al. I just prefer not to use it for anything but texting. I like doing things the old way. I like happening upon places. Serendipity."

"Dip me all you want, I've found the perfect café for our breakfast," I say, holding up my phone. "Do you have an idea yet for dinner and drinks?

Pete holds up a brochure. It has a beaming man and a woman sitting in a hot tub, a narrow cedar tabletop across the tub, and two pints of beer on the table.

"Pub fare and a massage okay with you?"

I start laughing out loud, and my laughter echoes through the room. People walking across the lobby are staring at me, but I don't care.

"*The Beer Spa?* You're not serious!"

"Oh, yes, I am." He grins. "And rules are, you can't say no. Besides, that's kind of rude."

"The place I've picked is tame compared to yours!" I chuckle as I read the brochure. "*It will cure what ales ya.* Ha! Good one. Unlimited pints? Twist my rubber arm. Let me go get my swimsuit."

"Great. Meet you back here in ten."

"You good, Legal Eagle?" Pete says as he serves himself another beer from the tap beside our tub. Whoever thought this place up is a genius. I'm seriously going to see if Dad can help me install a tap beside my tub when we get home, or maybe Trix can give me a hand with it. She's always been good with a drill. I'm more of a hire-an-expensive-contractor kind of gal.

"*Totaaaally relaaaxed.*" I breathe deeply through the steam and rest my head back on the small bath pillow at the side of the tub. "I didn't realize we'd actually be bathing in barley, hops, and yeast, but it's all good."

"The benefits of soaking in these all-natural ingredients are numerous," Pete says. "It's a very old therapy. They say we shouldn't shower off for twelve hours after our visit, but I know how much you love your hot showers, and how our Withybrook stay deprived you of that. So, that's not going to fly with you, right?" He chuckles.

I smile, slowly shake my head 'nope', and close my eyes again.

He's cute when he offers up useful information like that. It's like I've got my very own reporter traveling alongside me. And yet, he seems to intuit when I need my space—my alone-time. I don't have many people in my life who understand me like that.

As if reading my mind, Pete leans back and closes his eyes, too. Soothing music is playing through the spa speakers. It's instrumental mixed with a few dolphin calls and the sound of waves crashing against the shore. We lie back in the hot tub in silence for a few moments.

"Have you two had enough to eat? Enough pints?" a tall waitress with a strong Czech accent asks us in a hushed voice.

"I think we're good, right, Al? Sorry I don't speak any Czech—all those consonants are hard to pronounce."

The woman smiles and gives him a wink.

"I'm stuffed. I might fall asleep any minute." I open my eyes.

"You could towel off and go relax on a heated bed, if you want," she says.

"Oh, that sounds amazing." Immediately, I realize she said 'bed.' Not plural. Hormones, here we go again. Try to remain calm.

I climb out of the tub, walk down a step, and find Pete waiting there with a clean, black towel. I wrap it around myself and follow Pete and the Czech woman to a small, candle-lit, eucalyptus scented private room. There's a giant red hammock in the middle of the room. When I look closer, I realize it's just one big sleeping bag.

"Here you go. Sorry, the beds are taken, but this is super cozy. It's not very busy here tonight, so you can probably stay a half-hour." She closes the door and leaves us standing there alone in the near-dark.

"Uh, if you aren't comfortable, we could just go now," Pete says. He's staring at the hammock.

I need to stop running. He's not going anywhere for the rest of this trip, and neither should I. Be mature. It's just a hammock. "It's big enough for the both of us. I think we should go for it."

"What?"

"We were supposed to complete these outings without backing out, right?" I say, surprising myself once again.

"Yeah, but, Al. You… you said let's just be friends."

"Friends can hang out in a hammock." I chuckle. "Don't be a wuss!" I start to climb in. "Holy hell. It's warm! Check it out!"

"This is heavenly," he says as he slides in beside me. I check the ties on my string bikini and make sure everything's staying in place. At least he isn't in his boxer-briefs this time, but his bulging thigh muscles in those deep purple swim shorts have definitely made me want to lick my lips a few times.

"I may just fall asleep in here." He zips up the side of the hammock and pulls the top of the toasty warm sleeping bag right up to our noses. See? It's fine. This is fine. He's just going to fall asleep.

"We're in a papoose." I laugh. "A heated papoose. This is awesome."

Suddenly, I realize there's no backing out. I've literally got nowhere to run because we're zipped inside here, and I can barely move my arms. I turn my head a little to the left, and my nose hits Pete's chin. Oh, fuck.

"So. Looking forward to tomorrow when we find out what's in that envelope?"

I can feel his chest rising and falling as he breathes. I'm trying not to touch him with my hands, so I have them folded across my chest, but my left leg and his right leg are wrapped around each other. We're practically joined at the hip. If I just turn my body a little to the left, we'll be skin on skin from our chests down to our toes. Skin on skin in a hot, cozy hammock.

"Yup. I'm just going to sleep now, until that chick comes back to wake us," I say. Such a chicken. I'm such a chicken!

"God, Al." Pete breathes heavily.

I won't turn my head. I won't. I won't.

I turn my head, and he cups my chin with his right hand, bringing his lips inches from mine. "You're driving me crazy, you know that, right?"

He's driving me crazy, too. I'm driving myself crazy by resisting him. I want him, but, not here. Not now. Not smelling like barley and hops.

"Yeah, I'd like to take that shower now. Meet you out front!" I reach for the zipper and give it a yank, then crawl out of there faster than I can say hot hammock sex.

My hotel room shower has its own shower gel dispenser on the wall. I pump it three times and get a large dollop of gel in the palm of my hand, then lather it slowly across my tummy and thighs. A gorgeous lavender scent fills the room. I lean back against the glass wall and let the shower's warm spray massage my face, neck, and breasts.

Will we ever get to go back to pick Sandy and Nadia's lavender? Will we ever return? After all this running, all these mixed messages, can Pete ever forgive me?

He was silent the entire cab ride back to our hotel. He didn't look angry, or even confused. I couldn't make out his expression. He's never that quiet.

My thoughts are interrupted by a loud knock at the bathroom door. I turn off the shower and reach for my large, white towel. Pete comes in just as I'm done wrapping it around myself.

"Forgive me if I'm wrong, but I think you want me here."

He has two glasses of white wine in his hands. He places them on the black granite counter and walks over to me. I lean back against the glass shower door, unable to speak.

"You left the adjoining door open." He puts one hand at my waist and pulls me in close. My knees buckle. I'm quite sure my entire body has just turned to Jell-O.

"I'm done, Al. Done with getting close to you, and you pulling away. Done with you acting like you're afraid of me, when I know we've both never been more comfortable with anyone in our lives. I'm done with waiting.

"You feel it too, don't you?" He gives me a squeeze at the waist. "We travel well together. We both love beer and salsa verde. We both named our pets after political figures…"

"Those are just quirks. They don't mean we'll last."

"Who said anything about lasting? If you're looking for a lifetime guarantee, I can't give you that. I could die in a landslide tomorrow. Or Garrett might murder me. Look, I know Dan hurt you—"

"He didn't just hurt me. He screwed our marriage counselor," I say, tears welling in my eyes.

"What?" He steps back a little.

"Yeah. That's why we're divorced."

"God. I'm so sorry. I get it now. I get why… we…" He seems upset now. He turns away from me, leans against the counter, takes a big breath, then looks up at himself in the mirror. "I should go. I shouldn't have come," he says to my reflection in the mirror.

I wipe my tears, take him by the shoulders, turn him around, and wrap my arms around his neck.

"Don't go. Stay with me. Stay."

Pete

Chapter

Twenty

I can't believe what I'm hearing. She wants me to stay.

As I scoop her up in my arms and lift her onto the counter, three strands of her damp hair fall across her left eye. I gently sweep them off her face, resting my hand on her cheek as I pull her lips onto mine.

She's delicious, soft and inviting, but the power of this kiss throws me off balance. It's like I'm hooked up to a defibrillation machine. Every time our tongues touch, sparks fly up my spine, out my fingers, across my entire body, straight to my heart. I'm being shocked back to life. I can't stop kissing her.

She moans softly, wraps her arms around my shoulders, and pulls me in closer. God, it's hot in here, and my Levis and dress shirt aren't helping matters. The mirror and glass shower have completely fogged up. I pull away for a moment, take my right sleeve, reach over and wipe off a section of the mirror. She looks back at it a moment and smirks at me in the mirror. Dirty girl. She wants to watch, too.

That's the only signal I need. I start to unbutton my shirt, but she moves her hands up to mine and takes over, pulling it off and onto the floor in seconds. Her hands slowly caress my chest and abs, sending shockwaves up my spine. I pull her tight against me, and she wraps her legs around my waist, then starts to kiss that place where my neck meets my collarbone. Again, and again and again. *Grrrr...*

Tiarna cabhrú liom. Her tongue! Ever so slowly, her tongue dances down my chest. When she reaches my nipples, she licks them in a circular pattern, then gives them each a little nibble. I moan, inhaling slowly. Give me more. More.

I exhale, lift her chin, and look into her eyes.

"You good?"

"Mmm." She smiles, her eyes sparkling with an Allie look I've not yet seen.

"As long as you stay, I will be."

Allie

Chapter

Twenty-one

Pete's kiss is passionate, and his chest and his abs so delicious, but this room is so hot I'm finding it hard to breathe. Please, God, don't let me faint in the middle of steamy bathroom sex. That would just be wrong.

I lift my head off Pete's navel as I feel him start to wriggle out of his jeans and boxer-briefs. They're on the floor, and he's magnificent. I want to explore more. All of him. I reach out to touch him, but he lifts my head with one hand again.

"Patience. Sit back. Let me spoil you first." He pushes me further back on the counter. My towel begins to slip, and I nearly bang the back of my head against the mirror as he spreads my legs ever-so-slowly, then lowers his head. His tongue travels up my left thigh, rests a moment, flickers down and back up my right thigh, then up, up, up, oh, *fuuuuuck*.

So, this is it. I'm going to lose complete consciousness. Black out during the best oral sex ever. Figures.

As if he's read my mind, Pete grabs my ass, lifts me into his arms, and in one strong, sweeping movement, carries me out of the bathroom.

"Little hot in there, love. How's this?" He lifts me a touch higher, grins, and throws me backwards onto my white king bed. I bounce a little, then fall back with my arms high above my head, like I'm flying. My towel falls off completely, but I don't care. I'm so ready for him.

"Well, hello, gorgeous." He grins and climbs on top of me.

"Hi." I smile, and my eyes lock with his.

"You do realize, this is just part of my interview process," he says. "Allie Number Twenty-two is still an option."

I whack him on his upper arm, and he chuckles, then pulls the white duvet over us.

"Warm enough?"

"Would you just shut up and do me," I say.

He kisses my eyelids, my lips, my neck, and my breasts, over and over again. I relax, breathe out, and take him all in. We fit so well together.

I grab his shoulders and roll on top of him. He groans as I push my pelvis deeper into his, rocking up and down, up and down, arms stretched up and crossed behind my head. As I arch my back and push down forcefully, I notice him watching my breasts rising and falling, my tummy muscles contracting, my hair falling over my left eye.

"You are so beautiful," he moans.

I ride him hard and fast until I'm feeling breathless. He grabs my waist and rolls me onto my tummy, his sea-blue eyes bursting with desire.

With every thrust, he lets out a guttural growl. It's the hottest thing I've ever heard. The pillow I'm biting barely muffles my screams. He's hitting the right spot every single time. I'm going to lose it. I'm going to lose it. I'm going to... *Oh. My God!* Relief finally washes over us, and we collapse face-first onto our pillows, then turn to watch each other.

Our breathing slows, but we're still breathing in unison. Pete wipes his forehead, sits up, throws his head back, and starts laughing. What? I thought we were incredibly hot. What's so funny?

"Damn! We could have been doing that since Withybrook!"

The man has got a very good point.

"Well, we'll just have to make up for lost time," I say.

I sit up and wrap my legs around him once more.

Pete

Chapter Twenty-two

The morning sun streams through a crack in the hotel drapes, stirring me awake. I rub my eyes and roll to the left, reaching for a fluffy white pillow to curl into. Something else is there instead. Someone else. I smile at the first thought of her: Allie.

"Morning, love." I kiss the nape of her neck and pull her back into my stomach, spooning just as we did a few days ago. This time, however, there's no blanket between us. I love the feel of her skin on mine; she's so warm, and her hair and body smell like fresh lavender.

Allie turns over and opens her eyes. She gives me a quick kiss on the lips, and I close my eyes and pull her in closer, kissing her harder. She immediately responds to my insistent desire. Her tongue plays with mine as she caresses my shoulders and back, but after a few lovely, lingering minutes, she pulls away and jumps up and out of bed. When I open my eyes, I see her putting on her bra and a white t-shirt from her suitcase. As she's zipping up her jeans, she glances over at the laptop on her desk.

"Where are you going? Don't tell me you're thinking of working?" I ask.

She opens the laptop and wakes it up. "As a matter of fact, yes, I have correspondence on your case to do, so don't you go complaining." She chuckles. "But we also happen to be in Prague for just twenty-four more hours. So, get up! I want to see the city!"

I groan, turn face-down on the mattress, and pull two pillows over my head, covering it entirely. "Joan's treating you like her little paralegal, not the brilliant lawyer that you are, you realize that, yes?"

"I do. Hon, if it'd help you, I'd mop wet stairs." Allie smiles. "You did that for me."

"We could just stay in bed all day and watch documentaries about Prague." I pat the place beside me in the bed. "C'mere. It's not the same without you here."

"Smooth, but it's not gonna work." She smirks, heads to the bathroom, and shuts the door. "My app says it's best to get to the bridge by dawn. We're already late. Come on."

I try to remember that I love her get-up-and-go, but sadly, mine has gotten up and gone. I bury my face in the mattress. A few seconds later, I hear the bathroom door creak open, and the next thing I know, Allie's playfully jumping on my back. Damn. She's already found my ticklish spot.

The view of the Vltava River from this old cobblestone bridge is stunning. I have to admit, while it was quite a struggle, it was definitely worth ending our tickle-fight and getting out of that sinfully cozy bed for this.

I take Allie's hand and give it a squeeze, afraid I might lose her in this bustling crowd of tourists. Everyone's out enjoying the warm weather. There are dozens of hot-dog vendors, t-shirt vendors, painters, and jewelers lined up along the bridge's impressive 16-arch span. The sky's a celestial blue today, and the river's ripples shimmer with specks of light.

"Okay, hon, I know you love statues." She laughs, putting on her sunglasses as I inspect the fine detailing on one of the religious figures and snap a photo with my phone. "I read there are thirty of these statues along the bridge. We don't have to get a photo of every single one, do we?"

Hon. I like it. I could get used to that, although, I get the biggest kick out of her calling me McCarney. She hasn't said anything about the few times I've called her 'love.' I think that means she's good with it. Hope so. I don't want to do anything that could scare her away from me ever again.

"Nope, but only because I'm famished. Where are you taking us to eat?" I put the phone in my back pocket, and as I take her hand again, she grins up at me.

"Look at you, McCarney, actually using your fancy phone." She grins up at me.

"Photos and texts, possibly GPS. I'm an evolving man, open to change." I chuckle.

"The Beer Spa was brilliant, if I do say so myself, but you're the clear winner, Al. You couldn't have picked a better breakfast spot for me, although, it's making me desperate to text Terry and make sure Rosa's doing fine without me." I lift my cup of espresso and clink mugs with her. "Would that seem weird and needy to you?"

"You're a loving pet owner. She's old. I get it. Text yourself silly. I'm just going to sit here with this perfect little kitty," Allie says.

I watch her and take a mental photograph of her smiling in the sunshine as she pets the purring orange tabby on her lap.

This Cat Café—*Kočkafé* in Czech—has a dual role as cat shelter and restaurant. There must be at least 50 cats roaming the three rooms in this 100-year-old cobblestone building. Some lie on couches under the windows, others sit with patrons at the wooden tables. A few seem to prefer loitering behind the counter with the cook, or possibly, all that bacon.

Obviously, only cat lovers would truly appreciate eating with a feline at your feet, but there's more to this place than the kitties. This banana cake is scrumptious. I take another bite, then set it down so I can finish typing my text.

"Should we open the envelope?" I hold up the white note from our Maître D.

"I've already foregone staying in my individual suite," Allie says in a dramatic, deep voice, then giggles.

"That's a *Bachelor* reference, isn't it?" I chuckle and reach across the table for her hand. "I'm going to forgive you for that, because I lo—"

Oh my God did that just slip out of my mouth? Slow it down there. Slow it down. You can't be ready to say that yet. You've only known her a couple weeks. Don't be daft. You aren't ready.

Allie looks at the expression on my face and interjects. "I like you too, McCarney. Now let's open the envelope and see what he's selected for us to do today."

I rip open the envelope and read the card inside. Suddenly, I can't breathe. I start coughing, over and over.

Allie quickly gets up, rushes to my side, and slaps me on the back, hard.

"You okay?"

"I'm fine. It wasn't the banana bread. Look!" I pass her the card, and she reads it.

"Oh, hon. That's classic. Classic and tragic." She throws her head back and starts snort-laughing.

"We aren't doing it. No way. No fucking way!" I grab the card back, rip it up, and put the pieces in my coffee cup.

"Oh, way to wreck a memento. I would have put that in our scrapbook," she says, and I sneer at her.

"Allie Baldhart James, you cannot convince me to jump out of a perfectly good plane!"

"Whatever happened to you being an evolving man, open to change?"

How did this woman convince me to jump out of a perfectly good plane? How?

We're in a neon orange, white-striped PAC750 XL plane, 10 000 feet above the ground. It's almost time. It's almost time to jump! Bastard of a *Maître D who "meant well"*—Go n-ithe an cat thú is go n-ithe an diabhal an cat!

I'm standing with our diving partners Dalek and Beda, the cameraman, Jan, and Allie near the plane's closed door, perspiring like it's the middle of July. I'm rather certain my sweat glands are overreacting thanks to my nerves, but this badass royal blue jumpsuit I'm wearing over my clothes, plus my helmet, harness, parachute, and clear diving goggles aren't exactly the latest in breathable garments. It's searing hot inside this plane.

I don't actually blame Allie for convincing me to jump, and, if I'm honest, not even the Maître D. They just gave me a little shove in the right direction. I came to the conclusion on my own that this experience could rid me of both my nervousness around flying and my fear of abandonment. I'd be jumping out of a plane! Taking charge in the face of danger! I've never done anything this brave, or stupid, before.

We sat in that café for another two hours discussing the pros and cons. Allie showed me the web site for the skydiving company our Maître D suggested, and it mentioned that we could jump in tandem, with an instructor strapped to our back. That's when I slowly started to change my mind. After all, why did I want to take this trip in the first place? To do something out of the ordinary. To take a risk for once in my life. To face my fears. Skydiving fit the bill for them all, and Allie would be there every step of the way.

I was alone for a few minutes when she went to the restroom, so I typed out one of my infamous Pro and Con lists on my tablet. As usual it only had two pros on it: impress Allie and see Prague from sky. The cons included death, fear of death, and puking my insides out to death.

Allie never saw the list, of course. I may show it to her one day... if we make it out of this alive.

I can feel my heart beating fast inside my chest cavity, *ka thump ka thud ka thud*, all the way up to the middle of my throat. I take a deep breath and squeeze Allie's hand. Look at her: Smurfette in a helmet and harness. Damn, she's even cute in diving goggles. *I won't be Scaredy Smurf. I won't be Scaredy Smurf.*

Bloody hell, it's loud up here! I should have told her before we jumped. I should have told her, and now she can't hear me speak one damn word!

This one's for me, Dad, in spite of you. You left me, Evie, and Mum on our own without a word of explanation. You just left us. Just like that. The last people who saw you were two other drunks in our local pub. You never even said goodbye.

For years, I've wondered what it was that I did. Was I not good enough to make you stay? Were you not proud of me as a son? Is that why you left?

Well, damn you. *Go hlfreann leat!* I'm jumping today and leaving you behind me. I'm jumping today, forgiving you, and moving on with my life. I've got someone wonderful to love, and I know she won't abandon me.

Bollocks, I'm so fecking emotional, I can't catch my breath, and my instructor, Dalek, has just tapped my shoulder, giving me the cue that we're at 14 000 feet. Any second that green light by the door is going to flash, and we'll be off.

I look out the window at the Czech countryside: lush forests, expansive farmland, lovely little towns, a deep orange sun setting in the cerulean sky. Prague has enjoyed blue skies and gorgeous, above-seasonal temperatures all week. When Allie called the sky diving company up, the manager instantly knew us by our names. He said he'd happily take us at sunset, though they don't usually open until late March.

This is the chance of a lifetime, McCarney. Try to relax and take it all in. Thankfully, if memory escapes me years from now, our tandem pilots have GoPro cameras on their wrists; plus, there's an external cameraman taking a video for us. Excellent souvenir, but I hope the tabloids don't get a hold of the flash drive, or that someone edits out the part where I scream like a man-child for five straight minutes.

I swallow hard, take another deep breath, grab Allie, and kiss her hard. Our goggles bang together, and we have to pull apart. She's showing me that half-smile I love, but I can see the fear in her eyes. She's not the cool cucumber I expected her to be. I give her blue-gloved hand a squeeze, then lift mine and give her a thumbs up. She nods and does the same for me.

The green light flashes, the plane door opens to reveal a bright blue sky streaked with orange, and I don't hesitate. I've come this far, damnit.

I may as well leap! Plus, okay, Dalek is leaping, and we're attached, so I don't have much of a choice.

"AhhhhhhhhhheeeeeeaaaaaaMotherFuuuuuuckkeeeeeeer!"

I hear someone screaming, but I'm surprised to realize it's not me. It's Allie and her tandem pilot, a millisecond above me. Is she okay? This was supposed to be fun for her. God, please let her be okay.

Allie

Chapter

Twenty-three

Whoa, what a rush! This is amazing!

This is even better than that night in law school when I got up on the wooden bar with Trix; we danced for the crowd, and the bartender hosed us down with water.

I was scared yet excited about what would happen after I jumped up on that bar behind Trix, and now I'm feeling the same type of giddy anticipation and fear about what happens next.

What does happen next? Beda said we'll keep free-falling for a full minute, cruising at speeds I've only experienced on a roller-coaster. The earth below me is a blur of green and brown. It's map-like. I'm in a live version of Google Earth at sunset! We soar past clouds and a bright blue object to our right. I feel the cold wind on my face, tears coming out of the corners of my eyes, and the sound of my own heart pounding in my ears.

Suddenly, I realize Pete and his instructor, Dalek, are to our right. Their chute pops open, and a second later, so does ours. I laugh hysterically from relief and give Pete a thumbs up. He's not responding. He's looking straight ahead while his instructor struggles with some cords.

Oh my God! Their chute is twisted. Holy hell. I can't feel my heart beating any more. I think it's stopped.

They're falling faster than us. They're below us now, and Pete's instructor is still wriggling around. *JesusLordAlmighty I've been a terrible Catholic, but still, help them! Please!*

Why did I waste so much time with Pete? I liked him that first day we met. I knew I'd been wrong about him being self-important the minute I saw him doing the janitor's job. I knew he was kind-hearted and my type of quirky when he told me all about his cat, Rosa Parks. I knew he was a little bit broken, like me, when he mentioned his Dad leaving, and how he took over the farm to help his Mum. I knew, and yet, I waited until now to truly connect with him. Why? Why? Now we're both going to die jumping out of a perfectly good plane! I'm a total moron!

Oh. Wait. Dalek's doing what he referred to as a cutaway during our tutorial. This could be good, or very, very bad.

Their reserve parachute just popped up. *Oh my God, thank you. Thank you!*

Pete grins and gives me the thumbs up. I still can't breathe, so I exhale deeply and let out a scream of joy and exuberance.

"Yahooooo!"

That's it. I'm done. Pete's right about Joan. She's using me as her glorified paralegal. She only wants me back to do her filing and plan a stupid New Year's Eve bash. I can't do much more for him anyway, because of the conflict of interest. I'll send her that second doctor's contact info, which will safely fall under "limited legal services," but, enough now. Enough. I don't want to work for the firm ever again.

I know I have fire and passion, just not for corporate law. Look at me, up here on top of the world. I feel powerful enough to whoop anyone's ass. Screw you, Joan. Screw you! I'll make sure that you get Pete out of this mess, and then I'm done with you.

Shitdamncrapola, I hope I remember all that so I can email her when I'm safe on the ground. That was good.

Now, for Dan. Go ahead, asshole, marry that man-stealing-whore. Retire early. I don't give a flying fuck. I'm strong enough on my own. Me, the girls, and Pete, we're "starting anew," to quote Trix. I'm moving on.

It's time I used that inner strength to help the little guy—people who truly need my help. Trying to clear Pete of his charges has made me realize I'm ready to accomplish something much more meaningful than a promotion. Watch out world, here I come!

Woah, cool. There's the old city, and to the right of that, a large lake. I know that the sun is lowering below the horizon, but from my perspective, it looks like we're falling inside a giant orange. This is wonderfully, magically surreal.

I begin humming U2's *It's a Beautiful Day* as we continue to cruise the skies, then turn my head to look at Pete. He's got his arms spread wide-open like an eagle. I've never seen him smile this big.

Did I just think, "Me, the girls, and Pete?" Wow. It truly is a beautiful day.

"Lift your legs up!" Beda shouts into my ear as we approach the ground, and I immediately follow his instructions. Pete's already landed in a patch of grass several steps away from us.

Nooooo this feels too fast! Is this too fast? We're going to smash into the ground and end up in Humpty Dumpty sized pieces!

Shit shit shit! *MOTHERRRRR!*

Wait. What? I can't see anything under this parachute. Huh. That feels like grass under my hands. Oh thank God! We're here! We're here! We made it!

I unclip my harness, and Beda helps me up. He raises his hand to give me a high five.

"You did great, Allie! Sorry about the tangle there. Happens. All's well."

"You say that now, because we're both in one piece." I laugh and slap his hand. "Thanks, Beda! Thanks Dalek!" I walk over to him and we fist-bump. "That was so cool."

Pete's standing beside Dalek, his arms wide-open, ready to envelop me in a hug. I put my hands on my hips dramatically for a second.

"McCarney. We just got our act together. You wanna ease up on the near-death experiences for the rest of the trip?"

"I'll do my best, but I kinda dig the adrenaline rush." He laughs as he pulls me in close. I raise my chin and Pete gives me a long, passionate kiss, dipping me at the end.

"That was for the cameras," he whispers in my ear. "We gotta get our hundred and sixty euros worth." He smirks. "Now, I want you alone. Let's go celebrate somewhere private."

"How about dinner in the Old Town and breakfast in Rome?" I smile, remembering our itinerary. I've been the most excited about our 24 hours in Rome.

"We may just have tickets that'll get us there in time for your breakfast burrito and papers on our hotel balcony."

"After we sleep, or, don't sleep, love?" He kisses me again, and our electricity sends shivers up my spine. "Also, Burrito schurmito. I'm a new man. Evolved. Open to risk and change! I was going to look into Eurail, but after that experience, bah, a commercial flight's a piece of cake." He grins.

"This sounds like it's going to be quite the night. A late one!" I wrap my arms around him tighter and give him a squeeze. "You sure you aren't going to Cinderfella on me?" I giggle.

"Alas, I have no fairy godmother. There's only one bit of magic in my life, and I'm looking at her."

My knees buckle, even though I know it's a line. I love it. I love him. I wish I had the courage to tell him so.

He kisses my eyelids and mouth again, and I can hear Dalek and Beda groaning behind us.

"Okay, you two, enough suck face, time bus to town," Dalek says in broken English. "We order you limo for night, will meet us there. We heard favorite Czech radio station talking news. You need chaperone."

I realize he's saying the paparazzi have finally caught up with us, but I don't even care. I'm too busy kissing Pete back, anticipating our romantic evening and morning. I feel like I'm in a fairy tale, and that even though I'm a smart, accomplished woman, it's okay to run with it. It's okay to dream a little, maybe even a lot, and for once in my life, I trust the man I'm with not to crush those dreams. Bippity, boppity, boop. It's a fucking miracle.

The Ticket

Rome
December 31st
7 p.m.

Ouch. Last night, I felt like Cinderella-turned-princess, but tonight, I wonder if I've been wearing the wrong glass slippers all day. Make that, the wrong walking shoes. I thought my Go Walks were the perfect choice for touring Rome, but somehow I've managed to get blisters on my blisters.

I turn off the tap and lay back in the massive soaker tub. At least we're living in luxury here at the five-star Palace Hotel. It's close to everything, recently remodeled, and our suite has its own balcony. Pete just brought me a Chardonnay and turned on the fan so it wouldn't get too steamy in here. I'm thinking that perhaps he had an ulterior motive. His exact words were, "Save your energy, love." Perv. Love it.

Mmm, this Chardonnay is so sweet and refreshing. I take another sip, swirl it around the glass, set it down on the ledge, take a deep breath, and close my eyes.

What a perfect day. Pete decided to hire Luca, a car and driver/personal security expert, for the rest of our stay, and he suggested a VIP Skip the Lines tour which let us see the Sistine Chapel and tour the Vatican's secret rooms privately. We must have stood under Michealangelo's Fresco Sistine Chapel for half an hour, just holding hands and staring up, our eyes and minds trying to memorize every detail.

Next, Pete surprised me with a private tour of Castel Sant'Angelo, the Pope's Castle, built over Emperor Hadrian's tomb. They shut the museum down to the public so it was just the two of us for the entire afternoon, aside from Luca, who remained outside, and some staff who stayed in the main lobby area. We entered the castle-museum by walking up a beautiful 2nd-century brick-spiraling, covered ramp, sort of like a small train tunnel. We then toured several rooms filled with armor until I told Pete I was bored silly of looking at old revolvers.

"You can stay here, and I'll go walk around outside," I said.

"No, it's fine. Where you go, I go," he replied.

"We travel too well, hon. Aren't we supposed to have an argument right about now?"

"Why? I wouldn't want to waste any precious time with you. Besides, I've been thinking about you and me in that old entrance tunnel since we walked through it... it was completely empty." He raised an eyebrow. "The staff wouldn't go back there when they think we're in here, touring the rooms."

He raised his eyebrow even higher.

I looked at him and grinned. I'd been thinking the same thing for about an hour.

"Let's go back there, right now." I laughed and took his hand. We swiftly walked back to the tunnel, looking over our shoulders for staff along the way.

"You're quite the rebel, you know that?" Pete whispered in my ear, pushing me against the old stone wall inside the low-lit tunnel. It felt crazy to be doing this, but a good kind of crazy.

"Someone could come any minute!" I whispered as I slid my hands up the back of his cotton shirt.

"Yes, just might, love," Pete muttered into my neck, kissing and biting it lightly as he unbuckled my bra at the back.

"Pete! How will I put that back on in a hurry!" I laughed, then retaliated by unbuckling his jeans and unzipping the fly.

Pete reached his hand under my skirt and started caressing both my inner thighs, making me squirm in anticipation and moan a little too loudly. He kissed me hard, his tongue exploring my mouth, while his hands massaged my breasts. The old stone wall felt cold against my back, but his body, his mouth, so warm and inviting. I melted into him, wrapping one leg around his hip as he hoisted my leg up and pulled me in closer.

"Oh, God, yes, please," I moaned, feeling unable to wait any longer.

"Want you," he said.

I didn't close my eyes that time. I took everything in: the glowing lanterns, the curved stone wall, our open mouths gasping for breath in the darkness.

It was fast and furious, but oh, so good. We kept our moans to a low whisper, which only heightened our excitement.

"Yes!" we whispered together, a perfect release washing through us.

Minutes later, we walked out of the long tunnel hand in hand, passed through one empty room, and then strolled back through the main part of the museum, smiling at the staff as though nothing extraordinary had just happened. Pete slicked down the back of my hair as we pretended to study a glass-case of old daggers and revolvers.

"Enjoying all the armory?" a tall man in a staff shirt asked.

"Oh yes, especially the big guns." I giggled, and with muffled laughter, Pete pulled me out of the room.

Pete

Chapter

Twenty-four

"Ow. Ow. Ow. My blisters!"

"That's your fifteenth ow, Al. Not that I've been counting," I shout above the loud orchestral music. The hotel's gold and cream hued ballroom is small, crowded, and not air conditioned. The colossal sparkling chandelier above us dangles precariously from a gold chain that appears to have been crafted circa 1810.

I look down at Allie's face. She's in a stunning black strapless gown, but she's frowning, wincing, and looks positively miserable. I'm slightly less miserable, but I'm not big on tuxes, and this one is about half a size too small. I don't know if I've been eating too much on this trip, or if I ballsed-up the rental when I tried to speak Italian. The orchestra's off key, and the crowd is full of senior citizens falling asleep in their pasta. I want to be with Allie tonight—just not here.

"Crap. You aren't having any fun." She pouts, and looks over at a thin old Italian man attempting to do the Hustle with a walker.

"Me? You aren't having any fun! This was supposed to be your first ballroom dance, love, but you're doing more of a zombie shuffle," I shout, trying not to laugh. These dress shoes I rented are pinching my toes, but I dare not say anything about that right now. "Actually, the living dead from the Thriller video have a few more moves on you. I give them tens across the board."

Allie doesn't even laugh. She just stops dancing and mutters something under her breath. She bends down, takes off her high heels, and walks over to our circular dining table in the far corner of the room. There's another couple seated here for this elaborate New Year's Eve bash, but we've already discovered they don't speak any English. They nod at us over and over again, grinning like chimps at the zoo. Creepy.

Allie sits down anyway, and I follow suit. She's looking at her lap, her head in her hands. The orchestra switches songs. I know this one instantly. It's "The Way You Look Tonight."

I pull her chair closer to mine and gently take her hands off her face. "Like the song says, you look beautiful tonight," I shout, not caring that everyone can hear me. "Let's just get out of here."

"But, our romantic night!" Allie's lower lip wobbles. "I'm ruining everything."

"You're ruining nothing. You can put on some slippers, and we can dance on our balcony under the stars." I grab her heels in one hand and start to pull her up with the other.

"I'm not sure about the dancing." Allie winces as she takes a step toward the ballroom door.

"Fine, then we'll just drink under the stars. How bad could that be?"

Were these rain drops injected with some kind of growth hormone?

I think it might actually rain differently in Rome than in New York. It's been pouring sheets of rain for the last twenty minutes, and it doesn't look like it's about to let up anytime soon. Allie's sitting on the king size bed, wearing one of the white hotel waffle robes and white slippers from the closet. She looks adorable, as always, even though her mascara has run all the way down her sweet apple cheeks, and she's pouting. She has her back propped up against a fluffy pillow, her legs stretched out, and she's finally starting to look relaxed. I hand her a flute of champagne, and she gives me a half-smile.

"At least we're together and in Rome, right?" Even with blisters, she's got so much more inner sunshine that I do.

"Yeah, but I wanted the balcony dance." I frown, clink her champagne glass with mine, and sit beside her on the bed.

"Weren't we supposed to wait until midnight to drink?"

"To hell with that, it's raining, and the ballroom was a bust. We're bloody well drinking the champagne early," I say, and take another sip. It's bubbly, sweet and delicious. Looks like she enjoyed hers, too, because her glass is empty.

"Thanks for taking me to the ball. Sorry I was a pussy." She's massaging her feet.

"You are not a pussy." I grab the bottle on the night stand and refill our glasses. "Do you realize what you've done in the last year alone? You survived your husband cheating on you, won a few important cases while working as a single mum, and took a leap of faith to go on a trip with a strikingly handsome stranger." I smirk. "You told off your boss just the other day, and you like to have sex in strange places." I laugh. "You are no pussy."

Allie clinks glasses with me, then takes a sip. "Well, when you put it like that, maybe I should get a medal," she says. "And I didn't actually tell Joan "Screw you!" like I wanted to. I just said I was sure she was capable of sending out emails and putting up streamers on her own, and that I was having amazing sex with an incredible man and wouldn't be coming up for air anytime soon."

"You wrote that?" I have to put down my glass. She's unreal.

"I called her up and said it in person, late this afternoon." She giggles. "She was silent for a minute, and then she said, 'Good for you,' and then admitted she was overwhelmed with cases and hadn't thought to search medical insurance records to see if Garrett was treated by more than one doctor. She did the search. She's found something good."

"Really?"

"Yup. Garrett gave his lawyer the name of his longtime family doctor. He golfs with the guy. It's a cover-up. The doctor he saw for a case of whiplash the week before Christmas came clean when Joan subpoenaed his office. Garrett crashed his golf cart into a tree the week before your visit, Pete. That's how he got the whiplash. Nothing to do with you."

I can't help laughing. "What an ape. As useless as a lighthouse on a bog! He never could drive the bloody carts." I grab her and give her a kiss on the lips. "Al, you're brilliant. Thanks for helping Joan. I'm clear now... the judge won't cry conflict of interest?"

"Oh yeah, I was careful to stay out of what I had to. I just gave Joan a nudge in the right direction."

"Whatever are they going to do without you there?" I say as I pull back the top of her robe and start kissing her neck and shoulders. She relaxes into it, closes her eyes, and lets out a sweet little sigh.

"I don't know, and right now, I don't care."

"Ow. Ow. Ow. Okay, wait, right there. That's perfect."

I look down at Al's face, glowing in the darkness from the dozen tin candles I bought for us in the hotel gift shop. She actually told me it was unnecessary, and, I quote, "You're going overboard, McCarney."

I ignored her. Every woman I've ever met wants the candles, and now she doesn't want the candles? I'm confused. Do women have secret annual meetings where they change the rules just to mess with us?

It's finally ten minutes to midnight, New York time, and after making love, napping, and taking a glorious bubble bath together, Al and I decided to try dancing after all. I found my purple iPod, but forgot to pack my mini-speakers, so we're sharing a pair of ear buds—I have one in my left ear, and she has the other in her right.

"It's falling out again," she chuckles, and I help her adjust both our ear buds so James Taylor's smooth, buttery, *You've Got A Friend*, fills our senses again.

Never in a million years would I have guessed I'd spend New Year's Eve in Rome, waiting for New Year's to arrive in New York, dancing around a hotel suite in dress socks, with a blonde, barefoot woman on my feet. She just stepped up there, the first bar of the first song. She just stepped up, and I started turning to the beat of the music. We didn't even laugh about it. It felt natural, like we'd been doing it for years.

Lord, I could do this forever. I can't believe how close we've grown in such a short time. Am I ready for this? I've never kept a long-term relationship more than a year. Can I do this? Can I possibly manage to not do it all arseways this time? Maybe Allie deserves better than me.

"Pete! I need to turn up the TV. The ball is dropping!"

Allie steps off my feet, sits down, and grabs the remote. I sigh and sit down on the couch beside her. Bollocks. I've seen the ball drop in New York a thousand times, or at least, it feels like that. I could have danced close to her like that for another hour and never officially rung in the New Year. All I would have missed was a bunch of crazy drunk kids in overpriced hats sticking their tongues out at the camera. However, she seems content, sipping her champagne and smiling at Seacrest, so I'm not going to complain.

Allie also warned me that she'd get a call from her girls at about midnight, but I told her to stop apologizing. I can understand about tradition. I'm the king of routine and set in my ways. Besides, her family should come first.

"Ten, nine, eight..." Allie's calling out. She looks over at me and clinks her champagne glass with mine. I grab them both and put them on the side table. As the crowd roars "Happy New Year!", I wrap my arms around her and kiss her passionately. We relax into the kiss, resting our heads back on the soft couch. I feel her lips moving upward into a small smile and kiss her harder. I can't remember ever feeling like this. I can't even remember the last New Year's Eve when I wanted to stay up past midnight, let alone pull an all-nighter like we have. Allie's changed everything in such a short time.

"Happy New Year, McCarney."

"Happy New Year, love," I reply in a near-whisper. I cup her face with my hand. "And something else..."

"Facetime from EmKay Facetime from EmKay."

That's Allie's cell. Bollocks. Excellent timing. Just. Excellent.

"Sorry, hon, need to grab this! The girls will be disappointed. We always wish each other Happy New Year after the ball drops, no matter what."

Allie pulls away from me and grabs her phone off the coffee table.

"Happy New Year sweethearts!" she answers joyfully as soon as she presses accept.

I'm standing behind Al, my hands on her shoulders. I smile at the girls, but they're not smiling back. Thankfully, or not thankfully, I can tell immediately that it's not about me. They both have red, puffy eyes, and Em still has tears glistening on one cheek.

"Oh my God, what's going on?" Allie asks.

"Mommy..." Kayleigh starts bawling.

Jesus. From what Al's told me, she's the one who's usually most in control of her emotions. I gently guide Al back down onto the couch in an attempt to keep her calm, despite that her girls are not.

Allie

Chapter

Twenty-five

"Kay, try to breathe and just tell me what's going on." I hold the phone up.

Kayleigh takes a deep breath. Emma wipes her nose with her sleeve and tries to slow her sobbing.

"Dad just called for New Year's with what he said was great news," Kay says.

"Great news? So why are you two hysterical?"

"Lori's pregnant." She sobs.

I gasp.

"There's more." Kay stops crying so she can get her words out. "They're getting m-m-m-married in a month! On Valentine's Day!"

"*Mother fucker!*" There goes my fucking New Year's resolution. I can't help myself. Besides, I should be allowed to break it out in emergencies. From where I'm sitting, this is definitely one of those.

"'Happy New Year,' he said. 'You're going to be stepsisters,' he said!" Kay opens her mouth wide and puts her fingers in her throat to express her immense disgust.

"They're having the baby in October! I bet it happened just before Christmas!" Em chimes in and bursts into tears again.

"Oh, this is too much." I turn to Pete, and his empathetic expression opens the floodgate. I start sobbing uncontrollably. I can feel the temperature rising in the room, or is that just my temperature? I need something to kick, then something to break, and then an entire New York cherry cheesecake to devour.

Who cares about the flab factor of my ass? My cheating ex is having a baby with his lover.

"No, seriously, I can't believe this. Dan never wanted any more kids! I did, but he didn't!" I try to compose myself. Pete hands me some tissues from the coffee table, and I begin dabbing my eyes, but the tears keep flowing, so the dabbing seems pointless. I'm holding a scrunched up tissue in one hand and the phone in the other. Despite that the two girls I adore are on the other end of that phone, I want to smash this plastic bearer of bad news into a million tiny pieces. Damn. I want to hold it together for my girls, I really do, but I can't be Super Mum right now. I can't even be Sane Mum. Murderous thoughts are consuming me. Plus, thoughts of cherry cheesecake, which is just weird.

Enough. I'm going to have to set aside my shock and rage to help the girls through this. Be a grown-up. It's what I have to do, for their sake.

"Kay, are Mum and Dad close by?"

"They're in the kitchen cleaning up from dinner. We had a good New Year's until Dad called," she mumbles.

"Okay. Girls, we'll get through this. I know it's not fair that he gets a new family and left ours. It's so not fair. I get that. But we're better off without him. You know that," I start dabbing my weeping eyes again, "and being an older sister to a baby might be fun, you never know." I'm trying here. I'm trying.

"Milly Morgan says her baby brother's poop was always bright yellow with little seeds in it," Em says.

"Ew. Gross!" Kay exclaims.

Pete chuckles a little and gives my free hand a squeeze. I'm so relieved that he's here for this. Hell, we've jumped out of a perfectly good plane together, and he survived a parachute tangle. Hopefully, he can help me find a way out of this tangled web of lies, deception, and conception, too.

"I have to go home. I'm sorry, but my girls need me." The Facetime call ended just five minutes ago, but I've already cleared out the closet, and I'm trying to jam my three pairs of shoes and a bunch of souvenirs into a suitcase that seems to have shrunk four sizes in a week.

Pete runs his hands through his hair and takes a deep breath before speaking. "Love, it's bloody six-thirty in the morning on the first of the year! We already have a flight to Bangkok at ten-thirty. I'm sure every flight to New York is booked solid, and any that aren't will have ridiculous layovers. Your parents said they'd keep the girls busy, and besides, the girls made you promise you'd at least spend a few days in Bangkok."

I stop packing a second to look up at him. "I did promise them, but I crossed my fingers behind my back."

"*A stór.*" Pete's using his pleading voice, the one he rarely breaks out. "Stay with me a while longer. Please?"

"A store?" I ask, still sniffling. "Are you talking about shopping? What are you saying?"

"Oh," he hesitates, "I didn't realize what I'd said, but, it certainly fits." He blushes. "Treasure. It means treasure."

"Oh." My knees buckle. Damn him. Damn him and his sexy Gaelic expressions. "Em said Bangkok was the one destination you wouldn't stop talking about before we left. Besides, the baby isn't about to pop out tomorrow."

"But I want to get home n-n-n-ow!" I manage to say between sobs and sit on my suitcase. It's still not closing.

"Sweetheart, come here, please. Just sit with me a moment." Pete takes off his black bow tie and throws it on a chair, then takes my hand and pulls me into his arms. He wraps his brawny arms around me, and even though it's a tight hug, I finally feel like I can breathe again.

He lifts me off the ground and onto the bed, and we lay our heads down on our pillows, facing each other. He's stroking my hair and wiping the tears off my cheeks. God, that feels so nice. I exhale and close my eyes. Maybe I could sleep. Sleep would be good.

Then I remember everything.

"He's having a *b-b-b-baybeeeeeee!*" I sob and turn my face into the pillow. "A living breathing *baybeeee!*"

"Hey, hey, it's okay." Pete rubs my back in little circles.

"It's not okay! It's not fucking okay! He's a lying prick, and he gets to have a baby?"

"Love, did you seriously want a baby right now, at this point in your life?"

I sit up, wiping my nose with the top of my arm. Gross, there's snot everywhere. I start chuckling.

"No, okay, no, and can you please get the tissues?"

He sits up, pulls a few tissues out of his pocket and hands them to me. "Here."

He's not even smirking. What a gem. My mascara's run, there's snot pouring from my nose, and I'm still tipsy from the champagne. I don't know if this wins me a Hot Mess in a Little Black Dress medal, but he's not turning and running. He's tucking my loose hair behind my ears for me while I blow my nose.

I compose myself, put the tissue on the side table, cross my legs, put my hands on my knees, and take another deep breath. Breathe in, breathe out. Try to relax. What was he just asking me?

"I don't want a b-b-b-baby, but it's just so unfair he gets to start fresh like this."

"Yeah, it is, but you're forgetting something. He's forty-six right? He wanted to retire early, you said? Travel the world?"

"Yeah, he was boasting about it to me the other day."

"Well, you and I have just seen three of the world's most talked-about cities. He can wave bye-bye to that idea for at least a few years."

I can feel my lips curling upward into a smile. I look at him. He has a point.

"Yeah. I doubt they planned for this. He refused to get a vasectomy with me. I guess he never got around to getting one with Lori."

"It would seem that way," Pete says and wraps his arm around me.

"So, karma. It really is a thing," I say.

"Karma is definitely a thing." He kisses my forehead. "You think you're tired from staying up with me tonight? Imagine them in nine months."

He's right. They'll be Sleepless in Spit-Up Land. A baby is a beautiful addition to a family, but Dan and Lori aren't prepared for this one bit. That does make me feel slightly better, and hearing the girls giggle over possible baby names at the end of the call was a consolation.

"I hope they call her Elsa," Em laughed. "Because her parents' hearts are frozen."

They've already decided it's a 'her.' Thank God that child will have my precious girls to watch over her, or him. Thank God.

Oh, I do want to see Bangkok. And we're practically halfway there already... and... he called me treasure. Treasure! A few weeks after my divorce, Trix ordered me a wooden chair with Chris Pratt's face on the seat. We laughed and laughed, and took turns sitting on his face and taking immature photos when it arrived, but I honestly wondered that night if I'd ever find someone as hot, charming, and clever as Chris seems to be. Now, I'm with a Gaelic god who calls me his treasure, and who wants to show me around the capital of Thailand.

I put my head on Pete's shoulder, and he leans back and guides us to our pillows.

"You okay? Want to try to squeeze a snooze in before we have to go?" he asks, pulling the duvet over us.

I curl into his body, burrowing my face in his neck. I'm too tired to answer.

Bangkok
10 a.m., January 2nd

What was I thinking? That was the longest flight of my life. We've been off our feet so long, the blisters on my blisters even had time to heal.

I follow Pete into the grand hotel lobby, pulling my suitcase behind me. I'm so jet-lagged, and from the look on his weary face, so is he. I just want to flop into bed, possibly after a hot bath.

I sit down on the black leather couch beside the large indoor fountain while Pete speaks with someone behind the front desk. Once again, he hired a car and security service and found us a five-star hotel along the banks of the Chao Phraya river—one that wasn't on our original itinerary, just to throw off the paparazzi should they decide to trail us here.

There were no photographers hounding us at Suvarnabhumi International Airport when our driver picked us up, but I saw our faces on the cover of a UK tabloid in a magazine store, so it wouldn't surprise me if some British paparazzi do some digging and find out where we're staying. There are only so many luxury hotels here. It's a matter of time.

Pete's walking toward me with a grim look on his face. "Bad news. The room's not ready yet, but we can leave our suitcases in their luggage room and tour a little while we wait. They said come back at noon."

"You're kidding me." I sigh. "I'm about to fall over with fatigue."

"Well, we could just find a café and drink coffee. The good news is the paps haven't found us here, yet."

"The paps are probably in their rooms, catching up on their sleep." I chuckle.

"Ah, are we a princess today?" Pete says firmly. "Because I left your crown in Rome."

"Okay, okay, point taken, let's get coffee," I say, and I drag my suitcase to the baggage room by the front desk where an attendant tags it, tears the tag at the perforation, and hands half to me. After Pete has done the same he gives me his hand, and we walk out into the bright sun together. At least we dressed for the warm weather. I'm in a white t-shirt and black capris, and he's looking handsome in his deep-red short-sleeved dress shirt and khakis.

"Where to?" he asks as he puts on his black aviator-style sunglasses. They suit him well.

"What? You didn't study your travel app?" I smirk. "I'm shocked."

"I didn't even install it yet." He laughs, and I roll my eyes, and keep walking.

Allie

Chapter

Twenty-six

"Uh, Pete, I don't think this is the fishing village." I'm holding onto his shoulders for dear life as our tuk-tuk driver rips around the corner faster than our friend Sandy in his little white electric car.

Our bodies lean far to the left, and Pete grabs my waist and pulls me back into the center of the tiny blue and yellow tuk-tuk. We're both dripping with sweat, and our shirts are sticking together. Sitting this close to him right now is so-not-sexy.

"Guess that GPS of yours isn't fool-proof, Legal Eagle."

"My GPS works just fine, the driver's taking us somewhere different! I know he gets commission to take us to different shops, but this is ridiculous!" I shout above the bustling city noise.

Damnit Auntie Em, we aren't in Kansas anymore. We've hit the outskirts of Bangkok. I wanted to check out a couple temples and the fishing village and try the floating market. This is a long, winding dirt street lined with several brick buildings that look like old factories. Where the hell are we?

I hold up my phone and shade my eyes from the bright sun. Phek road.

What the Phek?

As the tuk-tuk driver turns another corner, I brace myself and grab Pete's waist.

"Look at that, Al! There must be over a thousand of them!" Pete says in my ear, and I look ahead, past our driver, to see what he's talking about.

It's an elaborate open air market, and it's like nothing I've ever seen before. A sea of bright red, yellow, and orange stalls fills the streets, as do thousands of people, food vendors, and the sound of live music. I can hear the music loud and clear, but the streets are so crammed with people, I can't yet see where it's coming from. Six women in front of a stall of Thai silk dresses and delicate, hand-painted fans are performing a beautiful traditional dance. Our driver stops the tuk-tuk suddenly, and I lurch forward, nearly bashing my head on the back of his seat.

"Shop now!" He grins and opens his left palm. Pete gives him a tip on top of what he'd paid before and gets out. So, we aren't at the fishing village. Oh well, what can you do? Maybe later. For now, this is beautiful, and probably far less smelly.

Pete reaches out to help me down off the tuk-tuk, but I leap off by myself and head for the silk dresses and fans.

"Can we get something to eat first?" he calls from behind me.

Argh. I'm getting irritated with all this flying and eating and no sleeping or sight-seeing. Remind me to never become a traveling sales person.

"Yup," I say and point to a food vendor selling various meats on sticks, rolls, noodles, and even pancakes. It all smells heavenly, and I want one of each. It's pretty obvious that I'm jet-lagging and PMSing at the same time. I should probably eat something soon, before I bite Pete's head off.

Noodles, rolls, and two strong Thai coffees to go in hand, Pete gestures to a small park across the street, and I nod. It's almost impossible to keep my eyes on him and not spill my coffee as we make our way through the crowd of tourists in the market, but he looks back a few times to make sure I'm still with him.

"Here." He points to a green wooden bench at the edge of the park, and I instantly feel relieved that I can hear him better. "Let's eat."

I sit down beside him and take a bite of my rice paper spring roll. "Mmm. Authentic Thai! Yes!"

"Hopefully that pleases her highness," Pete mutters as he spins some noodles around his fork.

I give him a quizzical look. "Seriously? You're the one with your nuts in a knot."

"It's not me, Al. It's like I can't please you today, from the room not being ready, to the tuk-tuk ride—which I thought would be romantic," he says. "Maybe we should just go back to the room and get some sleep."

Oh, no. Dad often scolded me, "Allie wants what she wants, when she wants it." Am I doing that again? I'm never nice when I'm lacking sleep. Tears well in the bottom of my eyes. "Sorry. I'm not trying to act spoiled, Pete, I'm just exhausted, and I miss my girls. I feel like I should be home with them."

"So then we'll go home, fine." He doesn't look up at me.

I put down my roll and take his hand. "Look at me. Please? It's all about timing. You've got Garrett to deal with and finding new work, and I've got Dan…"

"You don't have Dan anymore, but you can't let it go."

I let go of Pete's hand. Did he seriously just say that?

"Let it go? If you mean him, I let him go ages ago, when I filed for divorce. But he's getting married on Valentine's Day and having a baby. It's bothering my girls, so it's bothering me. I don't want him back, if that's what you're worried about."

A light breeze wafts past us. It's utterly refreshing on this humid day, but it doesn't reduce the sudden tension in the air between us. Not one bit.

"I know you don't want to get back with him. I just think it's… it's in our way. You talk about him a lot. Maybe once they're married—"

"He's the father of my kids, Pete! I have to talk about him. He's going to have to be in my life, no matter how many times I dream of backing over him with a dump truck! He's not going away."

He's so quiet. This is weird. Maybe he doesn't consider me his "treasure," after all. Maybe it's just a dumb Gaelic expression, and it meant nothing. He doesn't feel how I feel. Oh, God, he doesn't feel the same way!

I open my coffee, take a quick sip, and instantly burn my tongue. Figures. This fucking day!

I set down the coffee beside me and run my fingers through my sweaty hair. He needs to know I've moved on... Tell him you were thinking about getting a new place. Tell him you want him to help you. Maybe even something closer to his place. Maybe even... Tell him. You have to tell him.

"Pete, my girls come first... they always will. Maybe we should head home. I'm sorry. So much has happened—for both of us—it doesn't feel right in my gut to continue on vacationing as though you don't have legal problems and a job search back home, and I don't have Dan problems and a job search... But, uh..." He's looking at me, finally, so I look right into his sad, intoxicating, sea-blue eyes, try to stop fumbling my words and go for it. "Well, maybe... I want to start fresh. I need a new place. Maybe you could help me find a new place... and then... we could..."

"Live together?" he interjects. "Jesus Allie, we've only known each other a couple weeks! Shouldn't we date other people first?"

No! Oh, this isn't going right at all! My heart's pounding faster, and I can feel my cheeks flushing red with anger and frustration.

I didn't mean live together right away. I need to make sure Em would be okay with it all, and Kayleigh, even though she's off to NYU this fall. I need to find new work, too, but I wanted him to be a part of that. Part of my new life. Obviously, though, with that kind of reaction from Pete, we aren't meant to be at all! It's over. I can't believe this is over! So. Over.

I stand up quickly and toss the rest of my lunch in the garbage.

"Date other people? For fuck's sake Pete, you're forty-four. I'm two years younger. I think we know what we want. Wait, scratch that. I know what I want, and you're an ass prick!"

"Did you just call me an ass prick?" He looks genuinely surprised and a little hurt. Shit. Me and my big angry mouth. I just can't stop it...

"Yes, and I was being kind. There are lots more words for you where that came from. Ass. Prick. Shithead."

"Oh, sure, that's mature Allie. Real mature. I just thought maybe we were rushing it! Living together? Would your girls be alright with it? And what about Rosa and King? It'd never work."

"It would never *work*? What kind of attitude is that from someone who was doing me against a wall the other day?"

Pete stands up, takes a deep breath in, and puts his arms on my shoulders. "Oh, Al I don't know," he says slowly, sighing with exasperation. "I didn't mean it like that…"

I don't know what he meant, but it hurt, and when I'm hurt, I've learned to shut down. Immediately. I don't want to feel like Dan made me feel that day. Never again.

"I'm going to buy a fucking gorgeous silk robe, and you'll never see me in it. Goodbye."

Just as I'm walking away, I hear a man call my name.

"Allison! Over here! Give us a smile!"

What? I turn my head and see a flash go off. Camera flash. Paparazzi. They're back. They've just caught us arguing on film. Fantastic. Just brilliant, as Pete says.

"I've had enough!" I call to Pete from over my shoulder.

The paparazzi want a scene? Fine. I'll give them a scene. I know I'm acting about five years old right now, maybe four, but I don't care. I just don't care. I'm exhausted, hot, and homesick.

"I just want the paps off our backs, and I miss my girls. I want to go h-h-home!" I stand in the middle of the street, shouting between sobs, and storm off. Mid-tantrum, I narrowly miss being run over by a speeding tuk-tuk. Yup, karma. It's a thing.

Pete

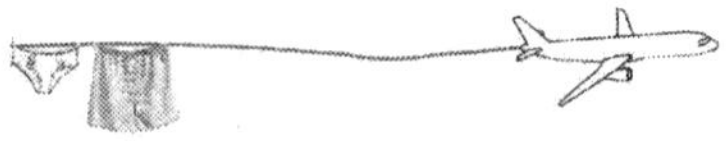

Chapter

Twenty-seven

I'm not running after her. No way. She's being far too immature to have her Prince Charming chase after her through an open-air market in Thailand. It's exactly what she wants, so she's not getting it.

My legs start taking long, purposeful strides, and suddenly, I'm chasing after her. I can't help myself. It appears that my legs know my heart all too well.

"Al, wait! Wait! I'd miss you if you went home! I'd miss you." I cross the street, calling after her.

It's no use. I stop running, put my sunglasses back on, and scan the stalls the length of the market. I can't see her anywhere, but I do see three fat paparazzi snapping photos of me from behind the dancing Thai ladies. Why are they even bothering to hide? Idiots.

Bollocks. Did I actually say that out loud to her, about dating other people? That was a knee-jerk reaction. God, I don't really feel that way. Why did I say that?

I lean against a brick wall and catch my breath for a moment. She's not really leaving, is she? She's just being dramatic, right?

I'd love to wake up beside her every single morning. The alarm would sound, and I'd tug off her ridiculous yet adorable *Ten More Minutes* satin sleep mask, kiss her passionately, run my fingers through her hair, and convince her to stay in bed another twenty minutes. But not for sleep. Never for sleep.

I'd love to re-discover New York with her. We'd visit old haunts and find new ones together. We'd go skating at Rockefeller Plaza at night, and I'd kiss her beside the glowing lights of that giant Christmas tree. We'd play scavenger hunt New York, and 'who can hail a cab faster?' and we'd visit all the cafés in one month and find our favorite, which, knowing us, would be a little-known mom and pop operation, not on anyone's 'It List.'

I know she wasn't really asking me to live with her. She was putting feelers out about the idea, and I bloody well went and crushed them and told her I wanted to see other women. Bollocks, I need to talk to her. Maybe she's on her way back to the hotel?

She can't go anywhere without her laptop and her suitcase. I'm going to have to hire a tour guide and get myself out of here, away from the paparazzi. Apparently, guides hang out here in the market to show tourists around using public transportation because they know the quickest routes. I'll hire one, and we'll head back to our room.

Wait. What if she's not going back to the hotel? What if she's wandering the market, lost? I can't just leave her here. I need to find her.

The second I look up, I see her. There she is, same side of the street, just up ahead. That woman!

She's with a tour guide already. Look at her, holding her cell phone like it's an extension of her hand—so damned organized and trendy with her fancy travel app. The short, Thai man with a balding hairline is nodding and smiling at her. She's nodding back, and when she looks my way, she sees me waving madly at her, but she doesn't wave back. She frowns, tucks a loose strand of hair behind her ear, then turns and walks off with the man.

That's it. She's being an infant, but I set her off. I'm running after her and ending this ludicrous argument once and for all. I'm bloody telling her, in the middle of a street in Bangkok. I'll shout my love for her so loud, she'll forget any of this happened today.

A dull roar rumbles in the distance, and the crumbling sound of bricks crashing to the ground thunders through the air. Not just some bricks. Thousands.

Shrill, heart-arresting screeches of human beings, big and small, young and old, pierce through the chaos. I can't understand the words, but it's universally understood. They're screaming in pure terror. *Tiarna cabhrú linn!*

Debris is falling from the sky; stalls are crashing down around me. There's dust everywhere, and a blur of people are screaming and running away from the market. I crouch low, cover my head with my arms, and run toward the chaos.

I have no idea what's going on, but I have to find Allie.

Heather Grace Stewart

Chapter

Twenty-eight

Tiarna cabhrú liom!

Al's trapped in there, under all that rubble. How am I going to find
her? I can hardly make out anything through all this dust and debris.

A woman in a Red Sox shirt runs past me, hugs a baffled-looking
man, and screams in English that a clothing factory collapsed two
streets over from the market. They run off together, but I stand still,
frozen in shock.

The wreckage has scattered here and several streets beyond us. There
are tiny bits of papers, clothes, and I can't even conceive of what else,
strewn across the ground. I see a tiny blue shoe on the pavement and
wonder if its small owner has survived. I can't see more than two steps
in front of me, and there's so much screaming going on, my ears are
ringing, but one sense is working: I'm feeling everything right now. My
heart is breaking.

My red shirt has become grey with dust from the sky, and the dust
continues to fall. I adjust my crooked sunglasses and look up to the sky.

It looks like it's snowing, on a hot, humid day, but the painful cries of people looking for their loved ones says otherwise.

That was the stupidest argument ever. I don't want to date other people. What the fuck was I thinking? Now she's trapped under part of a building, and she'll never forgive me. Christ, what if... what if...

I run faster, turning my head every which way, calling her name at the top of my lungs.

"Allie! Al!"

This is pointless. Everyone is doing the same thing. It's pandemonium. I stop, pull out my cell phone, and dial her number. She was just here. Just here with that guide. Surely, they hadn't gotten far, and she always leaves her phone on. I'll hear it ring.

I'm hearing a ring alright, along with about 20 other phones. They're coming from every fallen stall, all along the sidewalk, for four or five blocks. The stupid Christmas ringtones people never bothered to change are the most ironic. *I'll be Home for Christmas. You can count on me...* Bloody hell. This is heart-wrenching and impossible.

Wait a bloody minute. Think, McCarney. Think. She set up that *Find My Friend* app on our phones! We did it together on the flight to London. I was too busy ranting about Garrett's unethical actions to honestly pay much attention, but I remember she said it would pinpoint our location to each other if either of us got lost on the trip. Jesus, never thought I'd have to use it. Not like this.

So I just press this here, and the GPS chip in her phone should broadcast where she is. Waiting, waiting, waiting....

As I stare at my phone, the hot sun beats down on me, relentless even in this human tragedy. I can feel the sweat dripping off my forehead. I wipe it off and look around. The sky dust is starting to settle, but people are still screaming, still running, still searching for loved ones. Just like me.

Yes. Thank God, there it is. A flashing, hot pink dot. That's my Allie. She's one street over.

I start running as fast as my legs can take me there. I've never loved my bloody cell phone with all its apps so much as right now.

I'm here, but this isn't her precise location. It can't be! All I see are piles and piles of bricks and dozens of people around them, sobbing. Everyone is hysterical, trying to pull people out from under the debris. I don't see many survivors. A Thai woman, holding her bleeding head, is sitting on the sidewalk. Just sitting there among the debris, staring into space, in shock. A crying child, not more than five years old, is wandering around in a tattered shirt, picking bricks up off the highest pile and throwing them, no doubt looking for her mother. I yearn to help them, and yet, I need to get to Al first.

No. No! Al's not in there. She wasn't that close to the building when it collapsed. Was she? Did the guide take her here?

God. No! How could this happen? How?

The dot keeps flashing, and I keep turning, desperately searching... Don't let her be under there... please....

"Al! Al! Where are you?"

"Pete? Pete!"

The voice is muffled, but it's hers. It's Al! I look down and find an overturned tuk-tuk and two people hiding under it. It's Allie and her guide.

"Love! Gabhaim buíochas le Dia go bhfuair mé thú!"

I quickly lift the tuk-tuk off them, grab her, and hold her tighter than I've ever hugged anyone before.

"Are you swearing in Gaelic again? Bollocks something? It's always gotta be about your balls, huh?" She chuckles in my ear and squeezes me back just as hard.

"It means thank God I found you, Al, and I think we should have it engraved on our rings." I look into her eyes.

"Pete." She gasps and looks back at me, tears welling in her eyes. "Hon. That's incredibly romantic and slightly stupid. Half an hour ago you wanted to date other people! You said we were rushing things."

"Half an hour ago, I was an idiot. Half an hour ago seems like a lifetime ago. Al, I could have lost you in this. I—"

"Pete," she pulls away from me, "I am so sorry I stormed off like that, and we have a lot to discuss, but not here, not now. Not like this. We have to help these people! Look at them! We have to help!" There's desperation in her voice. I can't imagine what she's been through, being so close to the building when it came crashing down.

I look at her from head to feet, taking in everything I almost lost, and notice her left leg is bleeding. It has a deep gash extending from the knee down to the foot. "Al, you're hurt. You should rest. C'mon, sit." I take her arm and guide her to a large, solid rock she can sit on.

The guide beside Allie puts his hand on her shoulder and points to half a dozen ambulances coming up the street. He extends his hand, and I take it.

"I'm Chatri. I speak English. I can help you to a hospital and get you home."

"Hospital? Home? No, no, we should stay." Al looks up at me with pleading eyes.

"It would be helpful to stay," Chatri says. "It's mostly women and children who worked here. It was a sweatshop. Everyone knew it was in terrible condition. No one did anything about it."

"God. I've read about this happening in Cambodia, but I didn't realize…" I look around at the dead and wounded people, feeling ill.

"There are factories like that all over Thailand, too, and the conditions are just as poor," Chatri says.

Allie stands up, fists clenched.

"These women and children—they need us. We'll get my leg fixed up, then we'll help find survivors." Allie stands up, fists clenched.

One look at the fire in her eyes, and I know I'm not going to get her to sit down again. Not for a long time.

I have never felt such a strong sense of community like this before. It's been eye-opening and soul reviving. The Thai people are coming together like nothing I've ever seen in all my years as a journalist. I've never been this closely involved in a tragedy. I've never run toward danger, and I've never felt so alive.

Al's leg is wrapped in a bandage. She argued with the first-aid workers, saying, "There are people who need you more than me right now!" Then she jumped off the back of the ambulance and finished the bandage job on her leg herself. Now we're helping lift bricks and debris away in a frantic search and rescue attempt before authorities arrive and tell us all to leave.

We pull one female worker out of the least-deep area of wreckage, and together, the three of us carry her to the ambulances. Luckily, she has rather minor injuries, and as she gets bandaged, I sit with her at the back of the ambulance, its doors wide open.

"What was it like, working at that factory? Do you think this is just a fluke, the building collapsing?" I ask her.

As Chatri translates the woman's answer for me, Allie grabs her cell and starts recording. I know how her legal mind works. It's unjust. It's criminal, really, and we both want to make it right. If we can't make it right, God damn it, we can at least try to make the world aware of the real situation.

The woman tells me conditions inside the factory were horrific. She was also forced to work while pregnant, with just one day of recovery after she gave birth before having to return to work, or she'd lose her job. A twelve-year-old girl we rescue tells us that her older sister went on strike with half a dozen other workers outside this factory last fall, and they were crushed by authorities, who shot them dead. These people are too afraid to fight back anymore.

"Well, someone has to fight for them," Allie says as she continues to film my interviews, anger in her eyes.

The way Al says that with such strength and conviction in her voice sparks something deep inside of me. I look directly at the cell phone as she films me, Chatri, and the twelve-year old girl.

"Maybe I can," I say. "This is news, happening now. It's not influenced by advertisers. I'm not trying to improve the ratings. I'm just getting the story. This is it. This is the real story."

Allie

Chapter

Twenty-nine

"There, that should be good for the night."

Pete's just finished dressing and bandaging my leg again. We're finally settled in our elegant black-and-gold-accented hotel room, but it's very late. I still can't believe any of today's events. We just turned on the news, and the death toll is rising: 200 found dead and more still under the rubble. If it hadn't been for Chatri's quick thinking, I wouldn't be here to laugh or cry about anything.

I stare up at the elaborate 'dragon in the clouds' painting on the ceiling as I lay back beside Pete on our bed. I'm trying to decide how to discuss what he said earlier. Wherever I look, the fierce dragon seems to be staring right back at me. It's like he's taunting me about my own bravery. Will I be bold about our next step, or will I run back to the cave, where it feels safe?

Rings. Engraved rings! I mean, holy hell, that was romantic. Pete took my breath away—all those Gaelic words directed at me, dust flying everywhere, the rest of the world in chaos as my world became more clear to me than ever before. It was like something out of a movie.

But do I want a proposal by someone who's just seen his life flash before his eyes, when I've just had a near-death experience myself? It's not real. It's not... he didn't really mean it, did he? He was letting the adrenaline take over in the heat of the moment.

"Pete. What you said earlier... about... the rings..." I sit up and take his hand. "Let's get us home to reality. Home to New York, and we'll try to spend time together with a million interruptions from my kids, Dan Drama, me trying to find new work, and you trying to start this new blog job. Let's try that for a month, and see if marriage still seems like the dream to you then."

There. I know it isn't romantic, but someone has to be realistic here. Someone has to use their head. I guess that someone's going to have to be me. I'm the one who knows. Married. Cheated on. He's just being a hopeless romantic. As much as I want to lie back and melt into those sky-blue eyes and his warm, strong arms right now, I'm going to try to resist.

Pete looks at me and frowns. "I'm not a hopeless romantic, you know," he says, and I try not to gasp at how he's taken thoughts from my mind. "I am a romantic, but I have hope for us that's realistic. We've been through a lot together, Al. We work. We're the puzzle pieces finally fitting."

"So," he squeezes my hands, "maybe we should stay a while longer and help these people. There's a real story here."

I sit up straighter. "You'd rather stay here in Bangkok, getting this news blog under way, than..." I don't even know what to say to him anymore. "Pete, I have a family. I've got kids. They need me. I loved helping these people today, but I don't think I have anything left to give. Not right now, anyway.

"Besides, you're confusing me. You sounded like you wanted to start a life with me back at home?" I get up off the bed and slowly limp to the bathroom.

"Al, no! No! I just meant that I think I've found what I want to do next. I think it could work. I was only going to stay if you wanted to stay with me. You're jumping to conclusions. You have no idea how I feel!"

He starts walking toward me, but I close the bathroom door.

"You don't know how I feel, and if you keep shutting doors and walking away from me, you'll never know, Allie Baldhart James!" he shouts through the door.

Shit. He's getting angry with me. He broke out the Baldhart.

He's right—I do keep shutting him out. Why am I doing this to such an incredible man?

"Just give me a minute to think. I need to think, please." I try to speak calmly through the bathroom door. I don't want to freak out again like I did under the hot Thai sun today. I want to make the right choice. I want to be fair.

I put the toilet seat down and sit there, head in hands, trying to collect my thoughts. I'm so fucking torn right now. Emotionally tired and completely torn. I would love to stay here and help Phailin, that sweet little twelve-year-old girl we met, her mother, and so many others. I'd love to find them legal help. But, I'm needed at home, too.

And Pete. God, I love this man. I love him! But he doesn't seem to know what he wants right now. He's all over the place with his emotions, just like me. I don't think this is the time for either of us to make life-changing decisions, let alone ones that involve fondant icing, place cards, and receiving lines. I freaking hate receiving lines anyway. Loathe them! Why can't you just greet everyone out on the dance floor?

I know—I'll call Trix. I need to hear her voice, anyway, after today's events, and she'll know what to do. She always does. She's my calming influence. Once Trix and I speak, I can sit back down and have a good heart-to-heart with Pete.

It's almost noon back in New York. She's on holidays, so if she isn't sleeping in, I'm sure she'll pick up once she sees that it's me.

I grab my phone off the counter and dial her number. It rings twice.

"Hello?" It's a man's voice.

"Brad?" I'm sure it's Trix's husband who has answered. Why's he picking up her phone?

"Hey, Allie. Trix can't come to the phone right now."

"Oh, okay. Where is she?"

"Al..." He's breathing funny. What the hell? Is... is he crying?

221

"Al," he repeats, his voice quivering. "She didn't want me to tell you. She made me promise not to ruin your trip."

"Brad, tell me what's going on! Tell me!"

"It's stage three. She has stage three breast cancer, Al. They're giving her a mastectomy on Thursday."

Chapter

Thirty

Thursday, January 7th
New York Presbyterian Hospital

"You're awake."

I take Trix's limp hand and smile at her. Her jet black hair is matted to her forehead. Her face is pale and bloated, her eyes half-open. She looks exhausted. Of course, three hours of surgery will do that.

"You weren't supposed to come, dumb biatch," Trix says groggily and gives me a lopsided grin.

"Yeah, well, you're friends with stupid people." I reach over and hug her, then place her left hand firmly in mine. "So, how are you holding up, sweetie?"

"Honestly, Al, it was the most dull day ever, until I got this email from Victoria's Secret." She reaches for the phone on the tray beside her hospital bed and holds it up.

"Now that I know it's Thong Thursday, my life has meaning again."

I burst out laughing. How does she retain her humor through all of this? How?

Brad walks into the room and leans in to give Trix a kiss.

"Hey, sweetness. I was just speaking to your doctor. They think they got it all out."

"Oh, thank God," I say and finally feel the elephant that's been sitting on my chest get up and go outside for a walk.

"They don't believe it spread to other tissues, but it was a big sucker," Brad says and takes Trix's other hand. "So, now we just have radiation."

"And a shitload of drugs," Trix adds.

"And a shitload of drugs," I say. "But, we've got you. We'll help you through this."

"I lost my fucking left boob," she says, not one tear in her eyes as she looks up at both of us. Damn, she's so strong.

"I wonder where it is? Like, maybe they threw it in a dumpster at the back of the hospital somewhere?" We all start laughing and weeping at the same time.

"My boob! My fucking boob!" Now she wipes a few tears, but continues to laugh.

"I know, hon." I reach over and hold her. "I know. It's so unfair."

"All your life, boobs just never give you a break. They're either too small, too big, or they get the crappy cancer," she says.

"Yeah." I give her a half-smile. She is just made of awesome.

"We're gonna beat this," Brad says, quickly wiping tears off his cheeks. "And you're going to have reconstructive surgery later. It's all going to work out okay."

"He's right." I squeeze Trix's hand. "Try to believe, okay?"

The room falls silent for a minute. Trix looks down at her gown, at her chest. I glance over at Brad, but he looks away. I know that, like me, he's trying not to cry again.

"You want more ice chips?"

Trix nods, so I hand her the cup of ice on her tray.

"I'll go see about your dinner," Brad says. "They said you can eat now, and then we have to leave you to rest." He gives Trix a smile and leaves the room.

"So, where's that pompous Pete of yours?" Trix asks as I sit down at the edge of the bed. I'd told Brad about the Bangkok building collapse, but didn't have time to go into much else.

"Ha! Yeah, okay, I was wrong. I guess you could tell from my texts that he turned out to be amazing, but, I left really fast, so I wouldn't miss your surgery. And…" I nervously tuck a loose strand of hair behind my ear. "I told him to continue his trip."

"You did what?" Trix sits up straighter and looks at me with a mix of shock and disgust on her face.

"Well, he still has two more cities to visit on the itinerary, and now he's got this idea for a news show that's focused on getting the truth, not on making money. I think it's fabulous, and so I told him I'd rather he focus on that. Not on me."

"You told him to focus on his work instead of on you?" She frowns. "Wasn't that where you both started? Aren't you both taking like ten-thousand steps back?"

"Well, wait. Let me show you." I turn on the news. It's noon, and the building collapse is still a top story.

"See? They aren't interviewing a single Thai worker. It's all American tourists discussing their outrage over their trips being ruined. Pete's doing it differently. He's started this news blog called *The Real Story*…"

"He can't do that at home? Sounds a little selfish." Trix doesn't look impressed.

"He's not selfish, trust me. He's been very, very giving with me."

Trix raises her left eyebrow and giggles. "Giving, huh? Yeah, I'm sure. I've seen the size of the man. His teeth. His tongue."

I bite my lower lip and try to ignore the innuendo.

"I got the first available flight, which only had one seat left. I didn't tell him about what's going on with you. I insisted he stay."

"Why'd you do that?"

"Oh, Trix, I just didn't want him to lose this great opportunity. I haven't seen him fired up like this in a while. Garrett really messed with his confidence. I didn't want to ruin his one chance to get his career back on track. I mean, he proposed, so we have to talk about that at some point… I told him I'd think about it." I look down at my lap.

"He proposed?" Her mouth is gaping open. I look back up at her and remain silent for a long moment. I can feel my face flushing red.

"Yes," I finally say. "In the wreckage, after he found me. In Gaelic…"

"Oh, Good God! That is so romantic!

"Yeah… it was…"

"And you told him you had to *think*? He's gorgeous, Irish, and you said he's great in bed. What's there to think about?"

"I don't know. Not much, really. I was just scared… after Dan…" I let out a sigh. "I guess it just took me off guard. Anyway, I'll see him in a few weeks. He's going to see if our friend Sandy will fly home with him from London, once his trip is over. He hates to fly alone."

"Uh, that's weird. So now he's selfish and quirky." She laughs.

"No, he really isn't Trix. He's wonderful. He's the best man ever. I love him! You know? I do. I really love him."

"And, oh, fuck, I've treated him so badly the last few days! I shouted at him in a public market, I shoved his proposal under a rug, I locked myself in a bathroom to think, and I haven't answered any of his texts for forty-eight hours. I've been so confused over what to do with us."

"You shouted at him in public? You and your temper! You need to stop pushing him away, Al. I've never heard you talk about Dan like that, and I was your maid of honor. Pete sounds like the best thing that's ever happened to you… besides me, that is." She grins.

I laugh, reach over, and give her a hug. "Tell you what. You get healthy, and I'll make sure we work things out, eventually."

"Is that a promise?" she asks, but before I can answer, we're interrupted by Brad entering the room.

"So we have tuna casserole mush and cherry Jell-O," Brad says. He's with a woman in a blue uniform pushing a trolley of food trays.

"Oh yay, it's Tuna Thursday, too!" Trix laughs. "This day just keeps getting better and better."

"Brad, honey," she looks over him and winks seductively, "if you sneak me in some Jack Daniels, I may just slip off my Thursday thong for you before visiting hours are over."

Chapter

Thirty-one

Friday, January 8th

The one-block walk from the bus to my house is miserable, but Kayleigh needed the car today, and I really needed to visit Trix. I exhale deeply as I turn the corner and realize I can see my breath in the frosty air. Crap, this is one cold afternoon. I miss Thailand's heat and food and woah! *Mother fucker.* I just lost my footing on a patch of black ice.

I manage to regain my balance before falling, compose myself, then continue walking up our front stairs.

"Careful, love, you don't want to fall and bruise that beautiful arse of yours."

I know the voice and love the man. I turn at the top of the stairs to see Pete smiling up at me, his bright blue eyes crinkling at the corners. His sandy brown hair is blanketed in wet snow, as is his black wool coat, and he's got that sexy, unshaven look about him. It probably means he's been up all night, but to me, he's achingly gorgeous. I catch my breath before speaking.

"Oh my God, you startled me. How'd you find me?"

"This is your house." He smiles.

"Yes, but I mean, how'd you know I'd be here now?"

"You left that Find My Friend app on. Cell phones are actually rather useful, as much as I hate to admit it." He takes a step forward. "Especially useful when people aren't answering my texts." His eyebrows furrow, but the next look on his face, one of empathy, says that he forgives me.

"How's Trix?"

Oh, he knows. "Get in, get in, McCarney—it's freezing out here."

We rush inside the house, kick off our boots, and wipe down our coats.

"How'd you know about Trix?" I ask, leaning back against the front cupboard.

"Come on. I care about you, Al. I knew something was up when you left like that, so I called your Mum. She told me everything."

"Ha! You and my Mum. She thinks you're adorable."

"Aren't I?" He grins and moves in closer. I can feel his warm breath on my neck. "Anyway, I took the next available flight."

"You flew alone?" I lean into the cupboard for support. I feel slightly dizzy. "You did that for me?"

"Of course I did. The trip is off." He puts one hand on my shoulder and plays with the ends of my damp hair. "I can do my blog news show from anywhere."

"I checked it out this morning. The stuff I filmed that day?" I say, breathlessly. "It has two hundred million hits on your blog already!"

"You've been spying on me?" He smirks and moves in even closer. His body feels so warm, the look on his face so passionate, so intense— I've already forgotten the cold.

"Hey, you've been tracking me, jerk who wanted to date other people!" I frown.

"Yeah. That. Well, forgive me for being a complete and utter arse. I guess we've both been feeling confused."

"Pete..." I look up at him and realize I'm completely done in for. I have no more ways to resist him, and I don't want to. "I'm so sorry I shouted at you in public, and I'm sorry I told you not to follow me. I needed some thinking time."

"I get it, Al. I get it. I thought I could plan for when I'd love someone again. I planned my career, I planned my mornings, I even planned a trip around the world, but I never planned on you. It turns out real love is bloody inconvenient.

"But I want it." He cups my chin with his hand. "I want real love, with its mess and its inconveniences, and all its ups and downs. I want you, *a chuisle mo chroí.*"

"Love someone again? You love m—" My words are interrupted by his lips and rough, unshaven face meeting mine. His kiss is strong and full of desire, and I let my lips and my whole body respond. I've kissed him hundreds of times, but every single time my knees buckle and my legs feel like jelly. Our love is intoxicating. I lean back against the cupboard and succumb to all my feelings. After a moment, I unbutton his coat and run my fingers across his chest, then wrap my arms around his back, pulling his body closer to mine.

"You're the pulse of my heart, Allie," he whispers in my ear. "Thought you knew that. Didn't think I had to say it."

"Well, we rinne mairgairlí cránach de!" I say.

"Ha! We almost did make a right balls of it." He pulls back a moment and laughs with me. "You've been studying Gaelic! Not bad!"

"Yes, a little on the flight home because, I love you too, like no one I've ever loved before."

With that, Pete sweeps me up and carries me to the living room sofa. Within seconds, he's lying on top of me, staring into my eyes, worshiping me like I'm some sort of goddess.

Well, aren't I? I'm the Goddess of Overcoming Everything, damn it, yes I am.

God, he smells so good, and I love feeling his weight and desire on me again. I've missed his face, his touch, his voice, his accent. As much as I've missed my girls, at this moment, I'm ridiculously elated no one's coming home until after supper time.

He takes off our wet coats and throws them on the floor, then pulls open my cardigan and begins kissing my neck.

"You may be strong-willed, Allie James, but you definitely aren't telling me how to live my life." He stops kissing me for a moment. "I'll bloody well follow you home if I want to. For the rest of my life, if you'll have me," he says and pulls a small grey ring box out of his pocket.

"Marry me, you testy Baldhart?"

"Yes! Yes!" I squeal, sitting up and kissing him before he even opens the box. I'm weeping and laughing all at once as he places a stunning princess-cut solitaire on my left hand.

"It's gorgeous, hon, but I sure as hell hope you didn't have 'Testy Baldhart' engraved on the ring!"

Pete chuckles with me and shakes his head 'no', then bends to kiss my lips, my neck, my chest. When his eyes meet mine, a sexy growl escapes his lips. *Grrrr…*

I almost start purring. Oh, yes, this is going to be good.

Chapter

Thirty-two

Christmas Day

"C'mere, King, we should get back home now."

I whistle for King, and he practically leaps after me, bounding through the snow like one of Santa's reindeer on steroids.

It was a massive snowfall last night, but we're not driving anywhere today, so who cares? Besides, it was the perfect Christmas Eve snow: fluffy, fresh, and full of promise.

If you'd told me a year ago what my life would look like today, I'd have smacked you over the head with an irate Jib Jab elf and called you a liar. It would probably be a dancing Joan, or one of her poorly paid interns. I hear they are so overworked without me at the firm, they've got three new interns running around like chickens with their heads cut off, and none of the partners are taking time off except today. Oh well. You reap what you sow. I don't pity them one bit.

At least Joan was competent enough to find even more evidence that Garrett's whiplash happened before Pete stepped into his home office. I still can't believe that dumbass Garrett posted about his golf-cart accident on Facebook and forgot to take it down! With so much evidence against him, he had to make an on-air apology and never charged Pete with assault. Of course, we made popcorn, and my honey sat back and gloated during the entire apology.

"Told you!" He laughed as Garrett stuttered during most of his statement. "As useless as a lighthouse on a bog!"

As I clip King back onto his leash, I look down at my shimmering engagement ring and smile. Everything finally turned out okay for me. Better than okay. It just took a while for all the pieces to fall into place.

Some days, I can't believe just how good my life is. I'm engaged to a brilliant, sexy man, we're planning our June wedding, and for the past eleven months, I've been a staff attorney at The Legal Aid Society of New York. I'm helping women who can't afford representation, I love my work, and I'm earning just as much as I was before. The best part is I could get a major promotion next year. Everyone at work wants me as president when our current one retires next year. For now, though, I feel content exactly where I am.

"Woof!"

King tries to tug me up the stairs to our front porch, but I pull him back a moment to admire our house. Pete strung up tiny white Christmas lights on the roof and our pine tree the other night. It was sweet, romantic, and hilarious all at once; penthouse-boy wasn't fully prepared for all that home ownership involves, especially stringing lights up on our farm house's two gable-roofed dormers.

"Bollocks! Who makes these bloody shite lights anyways?" he said as he placed the end of the string exactly where he wanted it, then watched as one of the bulbs came out of its clip and the whole string came crashing down.

"You don't have to do this, hon. It's getting dark out," I called up at him from the bottom of the ladder.

"I want to do this, love. Next year, I'm totally hiring someone, but this year, I'm doing this."

I laughed, and out of instinct, looked over my left shoulder to see if there were any paparazzi hiding in the bushes. Not one, thank God.

They followed us around New York for the first few months of our engagement, often waiting to catch Pete outside his new *The Real Story* offices downtown, but after a while, the buzz around our love story died down, and they never found out, or bothered to find out, that we've laid new roots in the country. I hope they never do.

I love the peace and quiet of this old farm house. While it's definitely not a short commute, it's a stress-free drive from here to New York. I can get to work by nine, visit Kay in her dorm over lunch, pick up Pete at work at five, and we're home by six-thirty for supper with Em. I expected Pete to have a hard time with the new lifestyle and routine, but he adjusted quickly, and he says that along with his new work, living on a farm again has him feeling more relaxed and more his authentic self than ever before. I know what he means. Like he said just last week during our morning commute, when you want something badly enough, you find ways to make it work.

"Honeys!" I call out with a chuckle as I enter the mud-room, "I'm hoooome!"

King makes a mad dash for the kitchen before I get a chance to wipe his wet paws. I swear he's singing and drooling, "Turkey! Turkey! Goody! Goody!" with every bark. Rosa strolls in to see what the fuss is about, then quickly turns on her indignant cat paws and walks away, unimpressed with our return.

I take off my boots, hang up my coat, and join everyone in the great-room, which includes a large country kitchen. Pete's at the stove in an apron, stirring a pot. I come up behind him and smack him on the butt.

"You should be barefoot. Then, this image would be perfect," I say.

"Hello, love. Now go away, or I'll burn the sauce." He leans over and gives me a quick kiss.

"Mmm, homemade cranberry sauce this year! You spoil me." I kiss him back, but before I leave, he hands me a wooden spoon with some of the sauce on it.

"Have a taste—see what you think. Or, do you need some fancy app to be sure?"

"I don't need an app, McCarney. I just need you." I wrap my arms around him. "Um, and those tickets you got us to Marrakech and Cusco," I add with a smile. "Can't wait."

"Me neither." He winks. I'm so excited that before our vacation in Marrakech and Cusco, we're headed to Thailand for a few days to officially launch Legal Aid Bangkok (LAB). I'm thrilled to be one of the international reps for this pro bono project and look forward to spending time with Phailin and her mother, who are back on their feet again, thanks to LAB.

"Mum! Kayleigh won't let me use her straightener." Em storms into the room.

"It was two-hundred and fifty bucks—she could destroy it!" Kay comes in after her, pouting.

"Ladies, is this truly the Christmas spirit?" Pete takes his sauce off the stove and gives them a disapproving look. I love that he hasn't been trying to become their best friend, although, I do know that they love him. They certainly spend a lot more time here at our new home than they ever did at our old place. That's probably because their alternative hangout is a stinky dorm, or a home cramped with screaming triplets in diapers.

Ah yes, the triplets. Karma had its wonderful way with Dan, alright, when Lori delivered three boys in October. 'Travel' and 'early retirement' are no longer in Dan's vocabulary, as the pair are currently up to their eyeballs in round-the-clock feedings, colic, and yellow baby poop. Mum has always liked the expression 'a tit for a tat,' and now I like to add "and shit for a shite."

Dad looks up from his turkey-carving and gives the girls a look. They're still glaring at each other.

"Why do you want your hair straight, anyway? Is it for *Jeff-ery*? You want to look *beauuuutiful* for *Jeff-ery*?" Kayleigh taunts her younger sister.

"Actually, yes, and if you listened to me for a moment, you'd understand that I have serious boy problems here!"

"Girls, I can't concentrate on the bird. I need quiet." Dad laughs, but we all know he's slightly serious. Brad leans in with a flashlight, like it's complex surgery. Mum rolls her eyes.

"Boy problems, huh?" Trix calls from the sofa. "C'mon, girls," she says, getting up. "Kay. Em. Mel. Bring your drinks, and let's talk about this in the bathroom. Al. Louise. Let's go."

Trix gives me a look, then grabs the bottle of red wine and three glasses off of the kitchen island, handing me one. She runs her free hand through her short purple hair and grins. I love the new look on her. I have so much admiration for her—shaving her head even though she didn't lose any hair with radiation. She just wanted to support all the brave women she's met along the way in this journey. Thank God, the last few weeks, she's been looking so healthy. We're coming out of the dark tunnel into the light, again.

I put my arm around her waist as the women leave the kitchen. We'll leave the rest of the meal preparations to the men. Boy problems trump turkey preps, every time.

"Thank you, dear Lord in heaven and all my angels, I'm finally allowed to drink again." Trix chuckles. "I'm bringing the wine," she says, putting one arm around her daughter.

As the six of us cram into the downstairs bathroom, Mum admires what I call a "horrific peach paint job." She then remarks that it's slightly bigger than the bathroom at our old house, and we all laugh. Trix lifts the wine stopper and pours me and Mum a full glass. The three girls start toasting with Christmas punch in their glasses.

"To family," Mum says, raising her glass.

"To family," we reply, and I know I'm finally home.

THE END

Strangely, Incredibly Good

Chapter One

Katherine 'Cat' Glamour, you need to snap out of this. You're a grown, most-of-the-time-mature, 38-year-old woman. But I think you've finally lost it. You've finally lost your mind.

I blink one more time to make sure he's really there. He stands about 5'11, with a tanned complexion, muscular build, and jet black hair. His sparkling green eyes would win my complete attention if not for his bright red gym shorts and cut thigh muscles. I keep blinking but can't take my eyes away from the elaborate Celtic tattoo on his right bicep.

Yup, my Wii Fit trainer has jumped out of my TV, and he's standing in my messy living room. There's a pile of unfolded laundry on the maroon sofa, a pile of unread newspapers by the glass top coffee table, and a Greek God by the Wii Fit machine.

I've got to stop meeting my sister for Cosmos at happy hour on Mondays. Clearly, I can't handle even one tiny, overpriced umbrella-drink anymore.

I drop the Wii Fit remote. The room starts spinning. Seeing cheesies and chocolate milk stains on my carpet, I really wish I'd cleaned. The 911 responders, or perhaps the nice straight-jacket people, are going to be coming any minute, and will think I'm a fat, middle-aged slob who lives with her grandmother. *Which, let's face it, Fat Cat, you are, you are – and that's probably never going to change.*

Tears well in the bottom of my eyes before everything fades to black.

My day had started like any other ordinary Monday.

"Mom! Mom! I can't find my pink hoop earrings, and the bus is coming any minute!"

I wanted to hop out of bed and help her, despite the disrespectful tone. Jenna is my first born, my baby-turned-18-year-old-fashionista, and I want to grab every moment I can with her before she moves out later this summer.

The problem was, I couldn't just hop out of bed. That would require energy, and a sense of hope. Which would require losing all this extra weight. At this point, I am starting to wonder if that's even possible. They say it can be done, but I feel so hopeless, so down on myself, all the time. I just don't know where to start. It's like I'm frozen solid: an ice sculpture left on the Rideau Canal, and the people passing by don't realize I'm stuck here. If I can't find the motivation to fold laundry or read those newspapers, I certainly can't start making healthy meals and exercising. Besides, I can't even make gazpacho. Even after following every damn word in *Chatelaine*.

"Jenna, honey, I have no idea where you left them. See if Grandma can help you."

"Oh, fine then. Grandmaaa!" Jenna bolted out of my bedroom and headed to the basement. Then, Alyssa was at my door, hanging from the doorframe; her thin, beautiful, not-yet-womanly frame swinging back and forth with restless energy. She kicked up a foot and practically vaulted into my room.

"Don't forget I have my gymnastics class after school tomorrow, and Jenna has art. So you can pick us up at the gym at six-thirty."

"I haven't forgotten sweetie."

"And Aunt Cicily's picking us up today, right?

"Yes. I have to work tomorrow, so we thought you could stay the night at Cici's. You'll have more fun with your cousins." I trusted my older sister, Cici, with my kids more than myself at times. She was uber-organized, to the point of having cubby-holes in her mud room for my kids as well as hers, and everything labelled in her kitchen cupboards. I hated to admit it, but I couldn't cope without Cici's help, and her visits to my money pit, er, home.

"That'll be fun. Um, I was just wondering, when you come get me tomorrow night, I was wondering if you *had* to wear a t-shirt and sweatpants."

"I don't think much else is washed right now."

"You mean not much else fits." She saw how my face fell and immediately covered hers.

"Oh God, I'm so sorry, Mommy." She sat on the bed and took my hand. "I don't know why I said that."

Alyssa always said she didn't know why she said things. She didn't know why she felt things, she just did. My girl who just knows things and calls it like it is. God, I wish I were more like her. But then I wouldn't have married a dipshit of a man and had her and Jenna, my angels from above. Sometimes, you can't win.

I'll never forget that day when Alyssa was seven going on eight, and we were eating cereal together before school. Out of the blue, she said, "Mommy, do you see pictures in your head, and then a little later, they happen just as you saw them?" She went on to describe how a friend of hers came limping into class just as she'd envisioned it an hour before, before her classmate had fallen and twisted her ankle.

It was then I realized she had the gift of foresight, and she probably knew a lot more about what was going on in my head and heart than perhaps even I knew.

Somehow, that made me feel safe. It also made me feel a little anxious. Can I do it? Can I lose this weight that hangs over me like a dark cloud every day, and be the mother I've always wanted to be? I've been given these girls as a gift. I don't want to let them down.

I squeezed her hand firmly. "Because you're frustrated, Lyssa. I get it. I can't do much with you girls. You know I'm working on it. You know this. "

I gently tucked a long strand of her lovely chestnut hair – just my shade, but thicker and healthier – behind her ear so I could see her beautiful face. "I'm working on it, Lyssa."

"Kay. Bye. See you tomorrow." She quickly pecked my cheek and looked down, nervously brushing off her plaid skirt and tights, though there wasn't anything there to brush off, and got up to leave.

"For your sixteenth birthday, honey, that's my goal."

She's heard that before. How many times am I going to lie to them? To myself?

As Alyssa left my bedroom, I heard the front door slam. Jenna had left for school, and for the night, without even saying goodbye. I was failing as the Mom and friend I'd always wanted to be to them, and I only had myself to blame.

As I shuffled into the living room in my black boot-style slippers and leopard print flannel PJs, I heard Gram talking very loudly on the phone with her friend Pat, or so I assumed. Then I heard her slam down the phone. I made my way into the kitchen and found her muttering away to a frying pan on the stove.

"With all the advances in technology, you'd think they'd design a 'Leave-Me-The-Fuck Alone' button for people who annoy the hell outta you," she grumbled and sat down with her plate of food at the kitchen table. "It was an automated message from the girls' school. Some creepy robotic female voice telling us the correct procedure for dropping your kids off, so you won't mess with the buses. Jeezus. When I went to school, teachers and principals actually knew how to write letters. With sentences, and punctuation, and everything!"

"Gram. I told you, we can get call display."

"Naw, can't afford it. Don't want to talk to anyone anyway. Shouldn't even answer the phone. You want eggs?"

I nodded, sat down, and started fiddling with my fork. Do I want eggs? Sure. Sure, and I'd also like to know how it came to be that I'm sitting here with my 91-year-old grandmother, we have a generation gap miles wide, and she's the only person in the whole world who sees me right now. Not my fat.

"What's buggin' ya, hon?" Her sky blue eyes conveyed such depth, such warmth, but her raspy voice and bitter tone betrayed that. All everyone ever saw was a curmudgeonly old woman who had outlived her children, and become a burden to her eldest grandchild.

That's not the case, Gram. It's not. Your body may be frail, but your spirit is as strong as an ox. Hell, I'm more of a burden to you these days.

"I'm losing the girls. Because of my weight. Because I embarrass them at school. I'm losing them." I tried to wipe away the tears with my napkin, but they kept coming.

"Not really. It's only temporary. You'll win them back. Besides, body image isn't everything. Well yeah, it is to teenagers, it's all they see these days. Photoshopped bodies on their phones, in their faces. But your girls know better than that. Deep down, they know you're just getting your shit together. You'll win them back." She was at the dishwasher, loading it, because I never had the energy to bend like that.

91-years-old. Something's going to have to change, Cat. My parents are gone, and Gram's not going to live forever. You can't ask Jenna to stay home after graduation to help you bend and lift things. You can't ask her that.

"You think? You think love should be a competition?"

"Honey, don't ask me about love, but life is a competition – with yourself – and only the bravest and strongest survive."

"Yeah. I know what you mean."

"Bacon?"

"No. Cutting back."

 I swirled my eggs around my plate in little circles. "Gram?"

"Yes, cupcake."

"Dieting isn't working by itself. You know I've been doing that for years, and I just can't get results. So, today's my first day at the gym."

"Well I think that's wonderful. Since Jimmy left, you haven't done a godamned thing to take care of yourself. Yet you do so much for your girls and me..."

"Oh, a little less since the pounds started creeping up..."

I was already overweight when I got married, and gained ten pounds almost immediately. I'm honestly not sure how I went from pudgy to overweight in a matter of years. I'd tried every Miracle Diet out there, but the only miracle that had come out of those efforts was my Amazing, Shrinking Bank Account. I felt like a fool for falling for so many of the oldest tricks in the marketing book, but it's not like those companies don't know what they're doing.

When you're large in today's society, you're not only a target of ridicule; you're also a marketing target. Even the healthy lifestyle options didn't sell you the staying power you needed to possess, alongside the product. I could have bought 100 Slap Chops and all the vegetables in the infomercial, but I needed to find the self-love within to do the chopping every night; to stick with healthy eating. *Yeah, I read that in an Oprah magazine. I knew all the theories. Applying them? That was another matter.*

Gram was right. I stopped taking care of me a long time ago. Most of my overeating happened late at night, in bed, watching TV. Those were the nights I felt most alone, and started thinking about the failure of my marriage, and all the things we'd left unsaid. We never did talk about little Logan. We never did.

When I'm honest with myself, I realize the marriage was doomed from the start. It was doomed that night in June, after my first year of business college, when I went to Jimmy Fink's house after a cheap date at Burger King, drank way too many wine coolers, and slept with him. I thought he'd make me feel better. An instant fix. Instead, we had to get a lot older in an instant. Or, at least, I did. I got pregnant. All because I was suffering from overwhelming guilt over a tragic event I felt I'd caused.

"Cat? Cat. You going to be gone all day?"

I looked at Gram, blinked a couple times, and realized I'd been staring into space far too long. "Oh, God no, Gram, just this afternoon. I'm going to the gym soon, then I'm picking up my paycheque at Walmart and running a few errands. The girls are going to Cici's after school."

"I've got bridge at Pat's this afternoon. See you later then. Oh, and Cat?"

"Yeah?"

"Knock 'em dead at the gym. Kick those skinny-assed gals right off the treadmill!"

Yeah, if I don't give myself a heart attack. Sure.

As soon as she left, I took my plate of food and scraped both eggs and some soggy toast into the garbage.

Ugh. This is gross now. I'll grab one last donut at Timmie's before I start this new routine. I can do this. But it's baby steps. Baby steps.

About the Author

Bestselling Amazon author, speaker, and poet, Heather Grace Stewart was born in Ottawa, ON, and currently lives near Montreal, QC with her husband, daughter, and three feline friends.

After receiving her BA (Honours) in Canadian Studies at Queen's University in Kingston, Ontario, Heather attended Montreal's Concordia University for a graduate diploma in Journalism. She worked as chief reporter of a local paper and associate editor of Harrowsmith Country Life and Equinox magazines before starting her own freelance writing and editing business, Graceful Publications, in 1999.

In 2008, she published her first poetry collection, "Where the Butterflies Go" (Graceful Publications, 2008). Reviewers call her poetry 'modern' and 'unconventional', the writing 'tender', 'heartfelt', and 'vulnerable'. Additional poetry collections include: "Leap" (Graceful Publications, 2011), "Carry on Dancing" (Winter Goose, 2012), and "Three Spaces" (Graceful Publications, 2013).

In 2012, inspired by the world's infatuation with online relationships, she wrote and published the screenplay "The Friends I've Never Met". Praised by Hollywood actors & producers as 'funny', 'clever', and 'innovative', the screenplay rose to Amazon bestseller status in 2013. In 2012, she also released "The Groovy Granny" (Graceful Publications), a collection of children's poetry, with the help of her then 5-year-old daughter who provided the illustrations.

Following her success of "The Friends I've Never Met", Heather released her debut novel, "Strangely, Incredibly Good" (Morning Rain

Publishing, 2014), a contemporary women's romance with an element of fantasy. A year later, the sequel, "Remarkably Great" (Graceful Publications, 2015) was published and met with positive reviews. "The Ticket" (Graceful Publications, 2016), a contemporary romance borrowing its premise from a well-known Canadian news story, topped Amazon charts and has been touted as being "fun and engaging".

In her free time, she loves to take photos, scrapbook, cartoon, inline skate, dance like nobody's watching, and eat Swedish Berries—usually not at the same time.

Visit her blog at http://heathergracestewart.com and follow her tweets on Twitter, her Facebook Page and/or her Instagram.